KARMA Doll

Novels by Jonathan Ames

I Pass Like Night

The Extra Man

Wake Up, Sir!

You Were Never Really Here

THE DOLL SERIES

A Man Named Doll

The Wheel of Doll

Karma Doll

KARMA

Doll

JONATHAN AMES

MULHOLLAND BOOKS
LITTLE, BROWN AND COMPANY
NEW YORK BOSTON LONDON

Mulholland Books / Little, Brown and Company
Hachette Book Group
1290 Avenue of the Americas, New York, NY 10104
mulhollandbooks.com

First North American Edition: January 2025
Published simultaneously in the UK by Pushkin Press

Mulholland Books is an imprint of Little, Brown and Company, a division of Hachette Book Group, Inc. The Mulholland Books name and logo are trademarks of Hachette Book Group, Inc.

The publisher is not responsible for websites (or their content) that are not owned by the publisher.

The Hachette Speakers Bureau provides a wide range of authors for speaking events. To find out more, go to hachettespeakersbureau.com or email hachettespeakers@hbgusa.com.

Little, Brown and Company books may be purchased in bulk for business, educational, or promotional use. For information, please contact your local bookseller or the Hachette Book Group Special Markets Department at special.markets@hbgusa.com.

ISBN 9780316576123
LCCN 2024941727

Printing 1, 2024

LSC-C

Printed in the United States of America

For Jason

The Buddha emerged from the forest, calm and magnificent. The villagers, drawn to his radiance and equanimity, approached him and asked: "Are you a god?"

"No," he said, sweetly.
"Are you an angel of god?" they asked.
He smiled. "No, I am not."
"What are you then?"
"I am awake," he said, simply.

—Buddhist parable adapted from the Dona Sutta

PART I

1.

THE ANCIENT-LOOKING DOCTOR, with half his face in shadow, seemed to be leering at me.

He was also busy drying his hands on his dirty lab coat, which had a smattering of bloodstains, more brown than red. For my part, I was sitting on his examining table, stripped to the waist, my feet dangling like I was a little boy. A little boy with a bullet in his shoulder.

It was two a.m. and very dark outside, and the only light in the room came from a weak bulb in the ceiling, fluttered at by a moth who had mistaken it for the moon and would be dead by morning. Of course, I knew about such things, having flown toward false moons all my life.

Then the doctor stopped drying his hands — at least he had washed them — and said, "You have an interesting face. Almost Jewish."

"That's what all the girls tell me," I said.

That made him smile, and I got a glimpse of old yellow teeth, which went nicely with his jaundiced bald head. Then he extinguished the smile and said, "What caliber is the bullet?"

"Caliber" sounded like "cali-*bear*" coming out of his mouth, and he spoke English well enough, flawlessly even, but did so with a strange Russo-Mex accent on account of the fact that he was a Russian Jew who had washed up in Mexico City in the early '80s when the Soviets were getting rid of their Jews, a bit of information he had already imparted to me — he was a talkative old man — and I said, "I don't know the caliber. It was a rifle."

"Hunting accident?" he asked, knowing full well it wasn't.

"Yeah, hunting accident," I said, and he nodded, smiling to himself, and began removing the flimsy gauze bandages I had applied to my shoulder. While he worked, his little pink tongue kept darting out from between his lips, wetting a small blister, which I tried to tell myself was a cut from shaving, but I knew otherwise.

He turned on a surgical lamp to better see what he was doing, and his examining room was a converted bedroom in a private, off-the-books hospital in Rosarito, Mexico, roughly forty miles south of San Diego.

I had crossed the border a few hours before, and it was the kind of hospital — an isolated old hunting lodge in the mountains above Rosarito — where you could pay in cash and not give a real name, and where you went for specific ailments, like gunshot wounds and bad DTs. I happened to be there for both items on the menu: there was the bullet in my left shoulder, and I also had a hideous case of the French fits from too much cocaine.

I could have detoxed off the coke in the States, but no American hospital would have treated me for the bullet wound without calling the cops, which was why I had crossed the border for medical attention. That and other reasons.

The doctor finished removing the bandages, showing a sensitive touch, and placed them on the little metal table next to the operating lamp. Also on the table was a tray of medical instruments and the syringe of morphine he had already shot me up with to calm me down.

From his lab coat, he removed a pair of black glasses that had magnifying lenses on them, and they looked like something I would have liked to order from the back of a comic book when I was a kid, if my father would have let me.

The doctor put the glasses on, and his brown eyes got all big and distorted, and he showed me his yellow teeth again, just to be nice, and then he bent over and studied the hideous mound that was protruding from my shoulder and looked ready to burst. It was the size of a grapefruit, and the bruising from the bullet's impact had painted it red, purple, and green, with some bilious yellow peeking through wanting to join the party. In the center of the colorful mound, where the bullet had entered, there was a black scorched hole, which I had filled hours ago with Krazy Glue to stop the bleeding.

The doctor let out a little whistling sound and took off his comic-book glasses. "There's a lot of fluid built up," he said. "Mostly blood and pus, I imagine."

"That's nice," I said. "Let's get the bullet out."

He grunted in the affirmative but then pointed a gnarled finger at my face and said, "I can also fix that. Five thousand more." What he was referring to and pointing at was the four-inch wormlike scar on my cheek, which I had gotten a while back when a meth head had cut me open with a hunting knife.

"That old scar?" I said. "What about the whole face while you're at it?"

The morphine had me feeling glamorous and glib, and I didn't expect him to take my question seriously, but he said, "You need a new face? Why? There are people looking for you?"

I didn't answer him, but there *were* people looking for me. Bad people. Dangerous people. And not all of them were cops. Which was another reason I had crossed the border, and while the doctor waited for me to say something, he went back to leering, which might have been his resting state, and his little pink tongue kept darting out to make sure his blister was still there. Not wanting to divulge anything, which was why I had come to this medico in the first place, I leered back, and it was a standoff.

Then he said, "Okay, don't tell me. People come to me because I'm supposed to not ask questions. But I do ask. I can't help it. I'm nosy."

Then he squeezed my wrist, gently, wanting to show me he was a warm person, a kind person, which he was and wasn't, and he said, "So for a new face I can give you a good deal. Ten thousand, on top of the five for the scar, plus other costs I told you already for the bullet wound and the drug detox."

"That's it? Fifteen thousand for a face?"

He shrugged and smiled, a smile of acquiescence, and said, "Okay. Ten thousand. Why haggle?"

He had misread my tone. He had thought I was being ironic and that I was negotiating, which I wasn't at all. I thought fifteen thousand dollars not to be me anymore was a bargain, a once-in-a-lifetime deal, and not just because a new face might help keep me safe from the people who wanted to kill me. It would be much more than that; it would be a chance to be free of the fool I'd had to look at in the mirror for fifty-one years, the fool who had followed me everywhere, wrecking my life every chance he could.

Of course, what I wanted — liberation from myself — was not something any surgery could ever deliver, but I was high on morphine and sodden with a lifetime of self-hate, and so I made the snap decision to get a new mug. At a discounted price. From an ancient, unlicensed quack with bad eyes and a herpes sore on his lip.

I said, "Sure. Ten thousand for a face. That's fair."

I didn't let him know he had been bidding against himself, and I figured he must have been desperate for the money to have lowered his price so quickly, but it was something else.

"You'll be pleased with my work," he said haughtily. "My training was in plastic, and you wouldn't think it now, seeing me like this, but I did an additional year of studies at the Royal London Hospital, in 1975, learning the latest techniques — I was the only Russian — and after that I was the assistant to the head surgeon for the Bolshoi. You've heard of it?"

"The famous ballet company."

"Yes, and it wasn't just torn ankle ligaments. The directors of the ballet — under orders from the Ministry of Culture — wanted the girls, especially the primas, to have the hooded eyes of Anna Pavlova, and the boys were to look like Nureyev, even though he was a defector. It was their way of saying, 'You can all be replaced, even you, Nureyev.' So, you see, young man, I'm a sculptor. Like Rodin. But with bone and muscle and tissue."

He said the *s*'s in "tissue" with the sibilance of a Brit, and he smiled again, showing off his little yellow teeth, and I realized then he didn't really care about the money. He *wanted* to give me a new face, wanted the chance to practice his craft — we all like to do what gives us meaning — and he said, "*So.* Handsome or plain, Mr. Lou?"

I had told the doctor my name was Lou but hadn't given a last name. Lou, of course, was a phony, and I had chosen it after a good friend of mine, Lou Shelton, who had died in 2019. If I had given the doctor my real name, Happy Doll, he would have thought *that* was the phony. But it was real — my parents hadn't thought it would be a joke — and it was in all the databases, and, of course, I didn't want the doctor to know who I was. I didn't want anybody to know. It was time to disappear for a while. But maybe someday I could go back to my life, the life Happy Doll had in LA.

"Handsome or plain, I don't care," I said to the doctor. "We can also stick with ugly. It's gotten me this far. But what do you suggest? You're the artist."

"Handsome," he said. "I'll turn you into Gregory Peck. I like old American stars. They were men. Now everyone looks like a boy. Don't you agree?"

"I hadn't noticed."

"My point, Mr. Lou, is that Gregory Peck was a man. *And* a fine actor. One of the greats. Played a Jew once. And I keep thinking you look Jewish. Tough and big but Jewish. With blue eyes, like Paul Newman. He was Jewish. Most people don't know that."

He was hot on the subject, and so I threw him a bone. "I'm half Jewish," I said.

"I knew it! I know bone structure. I know genetics. I know *Jews.* What's the other half?"

"Irish."

"Who was the Jew? Mother or father?"

"Mother. She died when I was born. I was raised Catholic."

"Still Catholic?"

"No. I study Buddhism. But I'm not very good at it."

"Doesn't matter. Your mother was Jewish, so you're a real Jew. Like me. The chosen people. But they left out a part. Chosen *to be hated*. So what do you think? Gregory Peck?"

"I did like him in *Moby Dick,*" I said. When I was in the Navy, they had played it several times, over the years, on movie night, and that image of Peck as Ahab, dead and lashed to the whale, his arm waving his men on to destruction, has always stuck with me.

"Yes, Peck was very good in that film," the doctor said. "One of his best roles. Or what about Tyrone Power? Because you're dark and still have your hair, I can also make you look like him. His nose went up. No one will ever think you're a Jew again, which isn't a bad thing. And Tyrone Power was a big star. Very big. He was Zorro. The Mexicans love him. They play *Zorro* late at night on the television. I know because I never sleep. Not for years."

"Let's stick with Gregory Peck," I said, and the doctor, a real cinephile, it turned out, perhaps because of his insomnia, smiled and nodded in agreement, with a twinkle in his eye.

Then he picked up a scalpel off the medical tray, and for no reason at all he poked his thumb with it and a pearl of black-red blood bubbled to the surface. He studied it with interest, then looked at me as if he had woken from a dream, and said, "Sorry, nervous habit."

2.

I WAS AT THE hospital, which was called Casa Feldman, for two weeks, and on the premises, for the convalescing patients, there were ten wood-shingled cabins: small one-room structures with a toilet, a bed, a chair, and a single window. These had been the cabins of the original hunting lodge, and the main house, also wood-shingled, which had a big wraparound porch with rockers, was where Dr. Feldman (first name Boris) lived and performed his surgeries.

He told me that a Tijuana gangster had built the lodge in the 1920s — Tijuana was about ten miles from Rosarito — and ever since it had been owned by those who made their living outside the law. At first it had just been a hangout, a retreat, which made sense: the compound *was* idyllic — set back in the woods, isolated, no neighbors, and sometimes, when the breeze was right, you could smell the ocean, coming up from the bottom of the mountain.

Then in the early '80s, the Tijuana branch of the Sinaloa Cartel took the lodge over and started using it as a place for its soldiers to heal their wounds, and the Russian doc was installed. After twenty years of servitude, he then bought the place from his Sinaloa bosses and still gave preference to their soldiers, but his doors were also open to other underworld miscreants. Like myself.

I learned all this because the doc would come to my cabin at night for what he called "intelligent conversation," though like most people who say that sort of thing, he did all the talking. But I didn't mind listening to his stories. He was lonely, and I'd had Oedipal complications — "daddy issues" in modern lingo — my whole life, which gave me a soft spot for old-timers, and so the doc would sit on the side of my bed and hold forth on movies and politics, his life in Russia, his life in Mexico, Jewish nature (anxious/creative), Mexican nature (stoic/loving), and so on.

But then one night, after I had been there a week, he suddenly put the focus on me and said, almost out of nowhere, "I'm worried about you, Mr. Lou. Being on the run. You can't live looking over your shoulder. It'll kill you faster than the men hunting you."

"I never told you I was on the run," I said. "Never said I was being hunted."

And he smiled at me, knowingly. Why else had he given me a new face?

A face I hadn't seen yet; the bandages wouldn't be coming off for another week, till day fourteen. But, of course, the doctor was right: I *was* on the run, and I knew it was going to be a nightmare. But just how bad a nightmare and how many people would die, that I could not have foreseen. There was also the woman. I didn't see her coming. I didn't see any of it.

* * *

The first thirteen days I was at the hospital, no other cabins were occupied — business was slow — and it was in my little cabin that I took my meals, prepared by the doctor's wife, Esther. She was a short, grandmother-like woman who seemed to be all bosom, and what she served was a mix of Russian and Mexican food — homemade pierogies and borscht one night, gorditas and sautéed cactus the next.

The doctor's son, Ivan, was also an employee of the hospital, acting as the maintenance man. He was a burly, lumbering fellow, around my age, early fifties, and the doctor told me that his brain had been damaged at birth. As a result, he was a mute — "un mudo" — with the intellect of a child, a very strong child, and so along with taking care of the property, Ivan, under the doctor's supervision, was there to help as muscle if a new patient, coming off the narcotics they had ingested, needed the straitjacket treatment.

In addition to his wife and son, the doctor had two Mexican nurses living full-time in the main lodge. They were older ladies, very kind and gentle, like nuns in a monastery, and one of the best things about Casa Feldman, along with the fair prices and good home-cooked meals, was that I was able to have my dog, George, with me, though I don't like to say "my dog" if I can help it. It doesn't seem right to think in terms of ownership when it comes to George — he's very much his own man — but the point is that Dr. Feldman's hospital was truly a full-service establishment: bullet wounds, plastic surgery, detox, and dog boarding.

The doctor himself had several dogs, small to midsize mongrels, and at first, George, a white-and-tan Chihuahua-terrier mix, who enters the ring at a lean twenty-four pounds, was a troublemaker: he's wildly handsome, with an athletic figure and large bedroom eyes, which probably causes a lot of jealousy in the canine set, and his modus operandi with other dogs, no matter their size, is to attack first and become friends later.

Fortunately, this technique worked well enough at Casa Feldman.

One by one, George assaulted the other dogs — quick jabbing bites aimed at the scruff of the neck — and they would fight back, though no blows or bites would actually be landed, and after a few rounds of this, George and his sparring partner, having gained each other's respect, would then, thoughtfully, and with a lot of decorum and fascination, sniff each other's rectums, usually followed by some gentle oral sex. Humans can learn a lot from dogs, and certainly the French have.

So, by the end of the first hour on our first full day, George was welcomed into the pack, and he was very happy at Casa Feldman. He delighted in having friends, and it gave me great pleasure, as well, to sit in the doorway of my cabin each day — with my face swaddled in bandages like the

Invisible Man—and watch him run around the dusty, tree-shrouded property, chasing after and wrestling with his new mates.

In fact, my heart swelled like a bride's at the altar as I watched him. But I couldn't help it. I'm one of those broken people who love their dog too much.

3.

YEARS AGO, I HAD heard about the hospital from a fellow cop back when I was in the LAPD. The cop, whose name was Beifus and who looked like a Beifus, had a bad drug habit and would go to Casa Feldman on his vacations to clean up his act, without having it on his record that he had needed to detox.

I had lost touch with Beifus after I left the force in 2004, but when disaster struck in every way, resulting in my having a bullet lodged in my shoulder, I tracked him down and found out that the hospital was still in operation. Beifus then made the call for me — the doctor only saw people vouched for by former patients — and George and I got in my '85 Chevy Caprice, crossed the border, and made our way to Rosarito.

This was late January of 2020, and what propelled me to seek refuge with the doctor was, at the time, the worst case I had ever been involved in. I make my living — if you can call it that — billing myself as a security specialist, which is essentially a private detective, and my undoing was a missing persons case, with the missing person being an old love I hadn't seen in years. Her name was Ines Candle, and after a few days on the job, I managed to find Ines, a heartbreaking junkie, in a homeless camp in Olympia, Washington, but that led, almost immediately and tragically, to her being murdered for a very large inheritance she was due.

It turned out, I had been set up by a man named Hoyt Marrow to locate her — to lead a hit man *right to her* — and this sent me on a seventy-two-hour coke-fueled rampage of vengeance. Normally, I hate cocaine, it turns people into idiots after the first line, but in my defense, I was using the coke medicinally to not sleep and to deal with various injuries, psychic and otherwise, and while hunting down Marrow, who had gone on the lam, I found myself, all coked-up, on a yacht in Marina del Rey with an old friend of Marrow's, a fat man named Jack Kunian.

Like Marrow, he was a pimp and a sex trafficker, but he also made money as a bagman for the Jalisco Cartel. I had been hoping Kunian would tell me where to find Marrow, but he was resistant to sharing information and things got violent. He had two bodyguards with him, and I hurt all three men very badly. Then, not thinking straight on the coke, I helped myself to sixty thousand dollars cash, Jalisco drug money, which was stashed in the yacht's safe.

After that, I tracked my prey to Joshua Tree, to a small house in the desert. There, in a shootout with Marrow and his accomplices, I left behind four dead bodies, including Marrow, but I also took a bullet myself: the bullet that led me to Dr. Feldman and his scalpel.

But avoiding the cops in California because of my bullet wound wasn't my only reason for crossing the border: Kunian and the Jaliscos would also be looking for me, and my coming to Mexico, the homeland of the cartels, was smart in a counterintuitive way. They would be searching for me in LA; they wouldn't think that I'd be wandering around Mexico, spending their cash at a Sinaloa-backed infirmary.

But that's where I was, like a flea in the armpit of the beast, and some of that Jalisco money had bought me a new face.

4.

THE MORNING OF MY unveiling, around eight a.m., someone arrived at the lodge — I heard a car pull up, which woke me. I was in bed with George — he was snuggled under the covers — and the engine of the car was loud. Then I heard a door slam and some excited conversation in Spanish. I got out of bed, went to the window, and caught a glimpse of the doctor ushering what looked like an extremely tall man into one of the other cabins.

Casa Feldman, finally, had a new patient, and I crawled back into bed. I figured that after the doctor got the man situated, he would then come to my cabin and take off my bandages, and I really had no idea, at that point, what to expect. For two weeks, only my eyes and mouth had been visible; the rest of my face was wrapped in white gauze. The nurses had changed my dressings a few times and some sutures had been removed, but they had kept me from a mirror.

Naturally, I was anxious to see what the doctor had done. As I had sobered up and detoxed, the insanity of my decision frightened me. I mean, I had always been wildly self-destructive, but to throw away my face on a sleep-deprived morphine whim was a whole new level of self-disregard.

I rationalized, of course, that the only thing Kunian had on me *was* my face, with its distinctive scar. He didn't know my name and there was no way he could find that out. I was a rando, a coked-out madman, who had shown up on his boat asking for Hoyt Marrow; and the people who could link me to Marrow, which was Kunian's only clue to who I was, had all died in Joshua Tree, including Marrow himself. But Kunian and his two men had seen me up close, and it was likely that I had been caught on video surveillance, which Kunian could share with his Jalisco compatriots.

So, like I said, all they had was a face. A face I had changed. Which was going to make it a lot harder for them to find me and kill me, maybe even make it impossible.

But that didn't mean I wasn't scared as hell to see what the doctor had done, and that morning, as I lay in bed with George, I started thinking that I should just get it over with and take off the bandages myself, but that's when I heard the screams, an old woman's screams.

I was slow to react, to register that something bad was happening, but then I got out of bed and ran outside, barefoot, in my T-shirt and boxer shorts, and I saw the doctor come flying out of the cabin he had gone into with the new patient. I watched him bounce once and land on his back, and I ran over to him, and he was unconscious.

Then I turned and looked inside the doorway of the cabin, and I saw the new patient, the tall man I had barely glimpsed, and he looked utterly gigantic, and he was naked, except for black underwear, and the doctor's wife, Esther, was trying to get away from him, but then he knocked her to the floor. Then he started strangling Reina, one of the old nurses, and I ran in there.

I'm six two, 190, and this fellow made me feel like puberty was just around the corner. He stood at least six nine and probably weighed close to four hundred pounds, with arms as thick as legs and legs as thick as telephone poles. His hairless torso, with big drooping breasts, was a weathered mix of fat and muscle, and he had long, greasy black hair, which went to the middle of his pitted back.

Topping it all off was a furrowed and acne-scarred face that looked like an old pit bull's, which is an insult to pit bulls, and this giant was obviously crazed on whatever drug he was coming down from, in a state of psychosis, and he didn't notice me when I came into the cabin. He was too busy throttling Reina's neck, and I looked for a weapon and picked up an old, hard wooden chair, like the one that was in my room, and I slammed him in the back with it.

My left shoulder was still recovering, but I'm right-handed and walloped him good, swinging for the fences, and the chair was sturdy as hell and didn't break. It annoyed the giant just a little to be hit with it, and he dropped the old nurse, who was still alive, and he turned to look at me with black eyes that had no pupils.

It was then I saw that the doctor's son, Ivan, was slumped in the corner of the room, and I swung the chair again and the giant grabbed it in mid-air, taking it from me like it was a toy. Then he returned the favor and slammed me with it, right in the chest, sending me through the door and onto my back, next to Dr. Feldman, who was still out cold.

The wind was knocked out of me — I was sucking for air — and the giant followed me out of the cabin, still holding the chair, but then he dropped it, seeing me on the ground, which pleased him, made him smile, and he squatted down and straddled me, planting his knees on both sides of my hips, like he wanted to kill me or make love to me, and it was the former, because he lifted his enormous fist into the air, then brought it down hard and fast onto my bandaged face, delivering a gruesome hammerblow, which caused a red explosion on the inside of my brain, and I heard a woman in labor scream as her baby crowned.

Then I opened my eyes and realized it was me who had screamed, and the giant was raising his fist to smash me again, but then the dog pack, with George in the lead, swarmed the big man, and he swatted some of the dogs away, sending them howling, and George was barking at him and trying to jab in and bite him without being cuffed.

But then the giant man, still straddling me, grabbed George by the scruff of his neck and tossed him away like he was nothing, like his life meant nothing, and I saw George cartwheel through the air, land funny on his head, twitch once, and go still, and a madness went through me, like a flame, a surge of murderous strength, and I reached up and grabbed the giant around his thick neck, pulled myself into an embrace with him, and bit off most of his left ear.

He screamed and rolled off me, holding the side of his head, which was spitting blood, and George was paralyzed or dead in the sand, and with the mangled ear still in my mouth, I picked up the heavy chair and brained the man with it, and he fell face-first into the dirt.

Then I spit out the ear, and one of the smaller dogs, Pablo, grabbed it and dashed off with it, like a prize, and I ran to George, screaming in my mind, *No, no, no,* and I knelt beside him, and he was still and dead, but then feeling my hands on him, he opened his eyes slowly and seemed dizzy, but maybe all right, not paralyzed, and I held him to me and started rocking like a disturbed child, a regressed reaction, which was a mixture of relief that George was alive, but also horror that I had killed again: the back of the giant's head was caved in, and the dogs had gathered around him and were licking the blood in his matted hair.

When my rocking passed, I put George down, and he really seemed all right. He had just been stunned by his awkward landing, and so I went over to the doctor, who was starting to rouse, as were his wife, Esther, and Reina, the old nurse, both of whom staggered out of the cabin, followed by Ivan, whose left eye was completely shut and already quite swollen.

I helped the doctor stand, and then he saw the big man on the ground, the dogs vying for the back of his head like it was a bowl of food, and the doctor's eyes widened in horror, and he shooed the dogs away, cursing at them in Spanish and Russian.

Then he knelt, unsteadily, beside the giant and saw that the man's skull was bashed in and that an ear was missing, and the doctor shook his head, like that part didn't make sense, and he put his fingers into the man's neck and held them there, maybe just to make the effort, but, of course, he felt nothing. No distant thrum of life.

He said, "You killed him, Mr. Lou?"

"Yes. But I shouldn't have. I could have subdued him."

"No, he was insane on amphetamines. He would have wiped us all out."

Then the doctor was looking at me funny and I realized he was staring at my mouth, and without thinking, I darted my tongue out and my lips were wet with the dead man's sweet-tasting blood.

The doctor, alarmed by the thought growing in his mind, then inspected the side of the giant's head, tilting the skull ever so slightly in his hands.

"Did the dogs do this?"

"No."

"Then what happened to his ear?"

"He hurt George," I said by way of explanation.

5.

THE DOCTOR JUST STARED at me — this business with the ear was too strange to take in, and so he dismissed it and said, "Never mind, let's get him inside, in case anyone drives up," and he gave Ivan an order in Spanish.

In response, Ivan grunted and came over to the body and stood next to me. He couldn't speak, but he could understand, and his left eye was shut grotesquely and already purple, though it didn't seem to bother him, and in the one brown eye, which glanced at me shyly, I saw a childlike sweetness.

Then, together, he and I grabbed the giant under the armpits, which were moist and disgusting, and as we labored to drag him inside — nothing is quite as heavy as a dead body — the doctor said, "This man you killed is a famous luchador, a wrestler known as El Diablo, and he's been here many times to detox. A terrible drug addict."

We crossed through the doorway and deposited the corpse on the floor of the cabin.

I said, "His name is *El Diablo*? Are you joking?"

"No, I'm not joking. He's a legend in lucha libre and they all have names like that. But he's not just a wrestler. He's also a contract killer for the Sinaloa. Diablo's killed many men. *And* women. He killed two wives and both times got away with it. He's untouchable. Let's get him dressed."

He barked orders at his wife and the nurse in Spanish, and they started gathering the giant's clothes, which were on the bed.

"Why dress him?"

"Because he's going to die in a car accident. He was never here. But we have to move quickly. And then you have to go. We may not survive this." Then he squinted at me. "Are you injured? You have seepage."

I realized then that my forehead and the bridge of my nose, where the giant had smashed me, were throbbing painfully, but I had been so adrenalized that I had felt nothing. I touched my bandages, and they were damp with blood. "I'm all right," I said.

"I'll take a look at you after we get rid of this," he said, motioning to the body, and Esther and Reina were struggling to put on the giant's pants, an enormous pair of black jeans, and so I squatted down and helped them, and when we got the jeans to mid-thigh, the doctor stopped us and pulled down the giant's black underwear.

Esther shook her head with disgust and said something scolding to the doctor in Russian, but, undaunted, he pointed at the dead man's shriveled genitalia and said to me, "See? This is why he's homicidal. Destroyed his manhood with steroids. It's why he killed his wives. Out of frustration. A great big man but not really a man. Most of the world's problems are phallic."

Then, done philosophizing and grandstanding, he waved his hand for us to continue, and we got the pants the rest of the way on. Then we put on Diablo's shirt — button-down, red silk — and squeezed his shoes on him — size 18 white espadrilles, no socks — and I had never seen such large feet up close before: the knuckly toes, with their thickened yellow nails, were as long as fingers.

The dead man also had a black baseball hat, with red stitched-in cursive writing across the front that said *El Diablo,* and I lifted his pulpy head from the floor and put his hat on, like dressing a doll. And I stared at the dead man, cupping his head in my hands, like a midwife but in reverse, and he stared back at me with the forlorn eyes of the newly dead, eyes that always seem to say, *Not yet,* and I pitied the monster.

Then I lowered his head down gently and my hands were all bloody, and the doctor fished car keys out of Diablo's pockets.

"These three can't drive," he said. "Come with me."

I stood up and wiped my hands on my boxer shorts, and we left the cabin and walked to the side of the lodge where there was a dirt parking area that held the doctor's old Ford pickup truck and Diablo's dusty gold-colored Cadillac Escalade. *My* car was down in Rosarito; I had taken a taxi to Casa Feldman, not wanting anyone at the lodge to know my license plate or VIN number.

The doctor handed me Diablo's keys, which had a Cadillac insignia, and said, "Near the top of the mountain, about ten kilometers from here, there's a spot where we can send him over the cliff. You take him in his car, and I'll follow in the truck and drive you back."

"Sounds like you've had this plan ready for such a moment."

"Not really. I used to think of killing myself up there," he said, without feeling, and I empathized but said nothing. The doctor continued. "They'll find cocaine and amphetamines in his blood, which will explain his accident, and every ten years, some drunk Mexican drives off that cliff, which means we're due, and the police won't think about it twice, and I hope he'll be so mangled, they won't notice that the back of his head is caved in…*or* that he's missing an ear."

He leered at me when he said that last bit, then got into his truck and drove over to the cabin. I followed in the dead man's car, and in the middle console was Diablo's phone, but it was turned off, which I took as a good sign. Regardless, there was little to no cell reception on the mountain, so it was unlikely that he had texted or called anyone, letting them know he had arrived at the lodge. We had to assume that people knew he was headed there, but not that he made it.

After I parked the Caddy, Ivan and I dragged the giant man out of the cabin and got him onto the front passenger seat. It was hard work, and I was sweating profusely.

Then I quickly went to my cabin to put on some clothing and shoes, and George was on the bed, on my pillow, as if nothing had happened. I thought of hugging and kissing him, but then I remembered my bloody lips, and before I got dressed, I went into the bathroom to wash my mouth and hands.

I could have taken off the bandages then, but I wasn't ready, and, also, the doctor was in a hurry to get rid of the body. But washing up went slower than I expected. Disturbingly, the blood around my mouth had seeped into the skin, rouging my upper lip, like I had been kissing a woman wearing lipstick, and it was hard to scrub off, but, finally, the blood came out.

Then I got dressed, which gave me an idea, and I went back out to the cars.

Ivan was in the truck, sitting on the passenger side, and the doctor was waiting for me by the Caddy. I said to him, "We better take off Diablo's shirt and hat. I'll wear them. And we'll lower him in the front seat, so that he can't be seen. This way if I pass someone on the mountain, they'll think it was Diablo who was driving. Alone."

"Yes, yes, of course," said the doctor.

I then got the giant out of his silk shirt, took mine off, and swapped it for his, which draped around me like a red tent, and I put on his hat, which was a little damp with blood from the back of his head. Then I said to the doctor, "You know, we've been rushing. Maybe we should wait till dark when there's less chance of being seen."

"No. His friends will know that he was due here now, this morning. The longer we wait, the more risk we take."

"Are you sure?"

"Yes. If the Sinaloa find out that the great El Diablo died under my care, they'll kill all of us. Esther, the nurses, my son. *You.* It has to be that El Diablo never made it here."

"All right," I said. "Let's just hope no one sees us."

"I think we'll be fine. There are only a few cabins near the top, so there shouldn't be many cars."

"If I do pass someone, I'll lower my head so they only see the hat and not my bandages. And you and Ivan head out first. I'll wait a few minutes. We don't want the cars to be seen together."

"I can tell you've done this sort of thing before."

"I've done many stupid things," I said.

"So have I," he said, smiling with the forced bravery of a man headed for the gallows, and he touched my arm, indicating we were in this together. Then, back to business, he said, "At the end of the driveway, turn left and up the mountain you go. Near the spot, I'll pull over. You'll see me. It should take about ten minutes to get there."

"Only pull over if no other cars are coming. That will be our most dangerous moment."

"I understand," he said. "This is like *The Postman Always Rings Twice* with John Garfield."

"I never saw it."

"Sorry. Silly of me to talk about movies. I must be nervous."

"Let's go, then," I said. "We have a dead man to kill."

6.

Just as the doctor had predicted, there was little traffic, which was reassuring, and I passed only one other car, ducking my head, as planned.

At first, as I ascended, there was forest on both sides of the winding road, forming a canopy. But then after ten minutes of a steady, twisting climb, the trees stopped, the canopy ended, and bright sunshine was revealed. On the right-hand side of the road there was now rock face and to the left was a precipitous drop into a rocky canyon, with an old guardrail acting as a deterrent, and in the distance was the Pacific, which glowed like a blue mirror to the sun.

Then I came out of a turn and the pickup truck was up ahead on the right, on the narrow dirt shoulder, and the doctor, watching for me in his rearview mirror, put his hand out the window. He was pointing across the road to the gap, with no guardrail, where I could send the Cadillac over the edge.

I drove past the doctor's truck, did a U-turn, and parked on the opposite shoulder by the opening. Should a car come by now, the jig would be up, and with my hands shaking, I got the giant into his shirt and hat and, using all my strength, I awkwardly positioned the dead man behind the wheel.

Then, with the door open, I leaned in and shifted the car into drive.

But that didn't do anything, and so I squatted down and pressed on the accelerator with my hand, which was enough to send the Cadillac lurching forward, and I leaped back, barely avoiding being dragged along, and the gold car, in a rush, went over the edge and down the sheer rock face, crashing into the sand-colored boulders a hundred feet below.

Then it flipped twice, like it was alive, and the sounds of the crumpling metal and glass were devastating, concussive, a thousand car crashes all at once, and then the pickup truck was swinging around, tires squealing, and I piled in next to Ivan, and the doctor floored us out of there, and we heard an explosion. Of course we kept going, and the doctor said, "I don't think we'll have to worry about Diablo's missing ear."

Hyperventilating, but trying to get my breathing under control, I nodded in agreement, and on the way back, we passed two cars. We had been very lucky in our timing: another minute and the first car we had passed would have seen the Caddy on the side of the road and me pushing down on the accelerator. But they didn't see it, the gods had been on our side, and soon enough we were barreling down the dirt driveway to the lodge, tucked away in the forest.

The doctor parked the truck, and for a second we all just sat there, stunned, and the front cab was filled with Ivan's primitive yet pleasant body odor, which smelled like onions and working in the sun.

I said, breaking the silence, "I think your scheme might actually work."

"Yes," said the doctor, "and now let's get those bandages off and get you out of here. I don't think you want to be interviewed by the police, should they come by, which I think they will."

"Right. Have Ivan rake the Caddy's tire tracks in case they do come."

"Good thinking," he said, and he told Ivan what to do in Spanish, and we all got out of the truck, and in the lodge, in the doctor's examining room, I sat down on the table while the doctor washed his hands. Then he delicately removed the bandages from my face, but before he let me look at myself and without warning, he shoved two fingers up my nostrils, twisted them violently, and reset my nose, which El Diablo had broken.

The pain wasn't as bad as the hammerblow, but it was horrible nevertheless, like having a firecracker go off in my head, and I nearly blacked out.

When I got a hold of myself, the doctor gave me a glass of water and said, "Sorry, but I had to do that. Your nose was on the right side of your face. Now it's in the middle again."

Then he walked me over to the mirror on the wall, and there was my new face, and I saw someone — *not me* — who had just been in a very bad fight and whom I recognized, but I couldn't remember from where or when.

And then it hit me, hard. Harder even than El Diablo.

The doctor, unwittingly, had turned me into my father.

7.

I REALIZED THEN THAT all my life I had been like one of those paintings, the kind where you remove one layer and discover that underneath there's been another image all along. My father had always told me I looked like my mother, and the few pictures I saw of her did confirm that, but then it turned out that just beneath the surface, lurking all this time, like the boogeyman under the bed, was Dad himself.

Shorten my forehead, take the large bump out of my nose and narrow the tip, dimple my chin, shave my cheekbones, erase my scar, pull the skin of the whole face tight like a drum, and it was welcome back from the grave, Bill Doll…whom I hadn't seen in thirty-three years, not since I was eighteen and joined the Navy to get away from him.

Then nine months after I shipped out, he died of alcoholism: esophageal ulcers in his throat burst, drowning him in his own blood. He had never been able to get over my mother's death, which coincided with my birth, a linkage he could never forgive, and seeing him there in the mirror, I felt my legs sort of buckle, and I got scared, like maybe he was going to reach for his belt. Because that had been our life together: poison for him, the belt for me.

Then the doctor broke my trance. He said, "Diablo damaged my work, but, overall, are you happy?"

"What?"

"Are you happy, Mr. Lou?"

I was all screwed up and thought he was asking me if I was Happy — Happy Doll — and I looked at him, terrified, but then realized the true nature of his question, and said, "It's a face. Let's get out of here."

This seemed to wound him, and he said, "I know it's not exactly Gregory Peck, Mr. Lou, but no one will recognize you now from your old life, if that's what you wanted."

"Yeah, it's what I wanted," I said, and I made to leave, but he had me get back on the examining table and, sulking a little, he applied some ointment and then a bandage to the bridge of my nose, where Diablo's blow had torn the skin. I felt like I was losing my mind, but I was also holding it in, like holding one's breath, and I kept my eyes from the mirror.

Back in the cabin, with the doctor watching, I hastily packed my bag, and from my other bag, a locked suitcase, I took out the doctor's money. My bill, he told me, was an even twenty-five thousand dollars, which I counted out for him, but I did it too fast — all the money was in hundreds — and I lost track.

So he started to recount it, piling the bills on the bed, and I left him to it.

I grabbed my two bags — one with the remaining Jalisco money, thirty-five thousand bucks, and one with my clothing — and I took George outside so he could say goodbye to his friends, and he dashed over to the pack.

Ivan was off to the left, raking the Caddy's tire tracks, and I threw the suitcase with the clothing into the back of the truck, but I put the money bag on the front seat.

Then I looked at myself in the large side-view mirror, and I was hoping he would be gone, but my father was still there, and, even though it hurt, I scrunched up the muscles of my face and moved them all around. Then I closed my eyes and rubbed and kneaded my face with my hands, trying to rearrange things, and when I looked in the mirror again, my father had somewhat receded, or so I hoped, and now it was more like there was a mean-looking stranger in the reflection. A stranger who had stolen my eyes.

That's where I'm hiding, I thought, and I blinked, and when I opened my eyes, my father was back, and I said to him, scared, like I was a little boy again, *Please, don't hurt me,* and then the doctor came out with the money in a pillowcase. "You overcounted by three hundred dollars, Mr. Lou," he said.

"Keep it."

"Are you sure?"

"Yes."

"Thank you," he said, and brought the pillowcase over to Ivan, who took it to the lodge, and then the doctor said, "Let's go, Mr. Lou," and I called George back and put his harness and leash on, and we climbed into the truck and left Casa Feldman.

On the way down the mountain, the doctor driving, we passed several police cars and a fire truck racing in the opposite direction — word had been slow getting down to Rosarito — and the doctor and I looked at each other but said nothing, and I thought of Diablo, his corpse on fire, just like his namesake.

* * *

In Rosarito, I had the doctor take me to the base of the three-story parking garage where I had stowed my car, and as he pulled the truck to the curb, I said, "Tell me again. What's your story?"

"He called in the middle of the night, very intoxicated, to say he was going to be needing a bed, and I prepared for his arrival, but he never made it. That's it. Keep it simple. I think it will work."

"It's half true, which makes it good."

"Yes."

"I'll call you in a few days to see how it's going, and we'll play it careful on the phone, in case anyone's listening."

"I understand," he said, then handed me a large orange-colored prescription bottle. "Morphine for the pain."

I looked at the bottle, grateful. "Thanks for this and…thanks for everything," I said, and I meant it. I didn't blame him for turning me into my father; it was inevitable.

"We Jews have to stick together, Mr. Lou," he said and offered me his hand, and we shook goodbye. Then George and I got out of the car. I removed my suitcase from the back and smacked the truck twice, and the doctor drove off.

Feeling sad to part from him, I waved at the truck in farewell, like a homesick boy left off at school, and maybe he saw me in his rearview mirror, but probably not. When you wave like that, when your heart feels something, the other person never seems to look back.

8.

THE BATTERY OF MY old Chevy was dead, and the garage attendant, a skinny young man with a tattoo of a small cat on his neck, called a friend of his, a mechanic, at an auto-body shop. While we waited, the attendant admired my '85 Caprice, its boxy strength, and said, "Un tanque hermoso," which I translated in my head as "A beautiful tank."

He also liked George quite a lot and rubbed his face into George's neck, which I thought was a bit much. Then he asked me about the bandage on the bridge of my nose, and I said I had walked into a door. I mimed the action for him, and he laughed.

Thirty minutes later, the mechanic showed up, and he also loved the Caprice — that era of Chevys is popular with car fanatics — and it took a minute, but then the engine turned over.

The mechanic's English was pretty good, better than his friend's, and so I asked him the best way out of the city and then to La Paz. I had to ask because I didn't have GPS — my phone didn't work in Mexico — and the directions the mechanic gave me were a little confusing, the first part, anyway, getting out of the city, but after that it couldn't have been more straightforward: Mexico 1 South for about nine hundred miles. I hoped the Chevy would make it, and after I'd given the attendant and the mechanic twenty bucks each, George and I took off.

I thought for a second of going to one of the tourist hotels on the beach and sneaking into the business office. There I could go online and check if there were any news stories about all the dead bodies I had left behind in Joshua Tree and if the San Bernardino Sheriff's Department, which had jurisdiction, was looking for anyone.

This had been on my mind at Casa Feldman, where I had no access to a computer or working phone, but I dismissed this idea of a hotel business center almost as soon as I had it. I figured I had wasted enough time dealing with the dead battery and that it wasn't smart to stick around Rosarito any longer than necessary after killing Diablo and disposing of his body.

So the internet would have to wait, and as I navigated our way out of the city, making a few wrong turns, I thought about all the people who might be looking for me: the San Bernardino sheriff; Kunian and the Jalisco Cartel; and now, if the doctor couldn't hold his water, I'd have to add to the mix the Sinaloa Cartel and the Rosarito police.

My life on the run was turning into a regular party, but I had thirty-five thousand bucks cash on my side, so I felt like my odds were pretty good, no matter how many people were on my tail, and I was headed for La Paz because Ines, my old love, had spent time there in her twenties, had told me all about it, and so going there, in my crazy mind, would be a way to be with her, and I was already in Baja, so why not? I could walk the streets of La Paz, feel her old echo, and pretend she was by my side. It would be a way to mourn her after her death up in Olympia, which had set all this in motion: this being on the lam, getting a new face.

I knew, of course, that going to Mexico City or Guadalajara would be better. They were large cities where I wouldn't stick out in any way, but La Paz wasn't dainty, either. It was a good-size tourist spot on the Sea of Cortez, and I could just stay there for a few days and then keep moving, and the vague plan forming in my head, as I tried to get us out of Rosarito, was to roam for about six months. I figured that would be the right amount of time for things to cool down. At the end of the day, sixty thousand bucks wasn't that much for the Jalisco Cartel and their proxy, Kunian, and after a while any manpower being used to find me would be diverted elsewhere.

So, I figured that by August of 2020 — it was now early February — I could safely resume my old life back in LA, especially with my new mask. And the same thing with the San Bernardino Sheriff's Department: in six months, if they didn't seem to be looking to pin Joshua Tree on anyone, I could go home.

As for the Sinaloa Cartel and the local police, I was counting on the doctor to keep me safe, which was risky. If he was pressured, if our scheme didn't work, he'd have to give me up. I understood that. Still, I was counting on him, and, in fact, I was counting on a lot of things to swing my way, a lot of luck, and then, finally, I managed to get clear of Rosarito and saw the sign for MEXICO 1.

George, sensing something, the beginning of a new chapter in our lives, put his paws on the dashboard and stared straight ahead, alert and beautiful, and I said, "Six months on the run won't be so bad, George. It'll be an adventure."

But he didn't have anything to say to that. As always, he was in the present, not the future, and so I pointed the car south to La Paz and the Sea of Cortez.

PART II

1.

ON MY FIFTH DAY in La Paz, I was in the non-touristy part of town, doing some heavy midday drinking in a little alleyway cantina. There were a handful of men in there, mostly older, and Mexican love songs were playing on the radio, but not too loud so as to drive you nuts.

I was sitting in the corner, by the window, where I could keep an eye on things, and sunlight, streaming with particles, was flowing past me at a steady clip. To amuse myself, I kept running my hand through the motes, disturbing whole universes, like a god.

A reckless god.

And maybe because I looked like my father now, I was behaving like him, drinking a lot, and after I'd had a few tequilas, this old-timer, an expat wearing faded khaki shorts and a Bally's Casino T-shirt, came up to me with a large shot glass of reposado in his hand.

He had sniffed me out as a fellow American — the place was for locals — and asked if he could join us at our table. The "us" being me and George, who was sitting straight up in my lap, using me like a highchair, and I said to the old-timer, "Sure, have a seat," and he looked like a sweet little guy who might have been midsize once but probably had been shrinking for a while.

He was certainly scrawny as hell — if he had any calf muscles left I couldn't see them — and I let him join us because I didn't perceive him as a threat: he was wearing flimsy sandals. Bad guys never wear sandals, because even old bad guys have to run sometimes. He sat down and offered me his hand. "I'm Vic," he said. "Vic Bingham."

"Lou. Lou Brink," I said, figuring it made sense to keep using my phony name, to which I had added a surname that I liked the sound of.

Then, introductions out of the way, we clinked shot glasses and drank, and Vic, up close, looked to be in his midseventies but could pass for mideighties. There was a meager white beard along his jawline, which was all he could muster, and he had a little wing of silky white hair barely holding on to the top of his head. On the plus side, his sun-faded blue eyes seemed merry and kind, even luminous, but the tip of his nose was veiny and purple, no oxygen there, and his neck was arranged in sun-damaged folds, like a fleshy accordion.

He said, "Where you from in the States, Lou?"

"San Diego," I said, which was true. It was where I had grown up. "Yourself?"

"Reno."

"Nice town," I said, lying, and we both knew it, but that didn't fluster him.

"Who's the pretty lady?"

"His name's George," I said, and I didn't sound drunk, but I was.

"Oh, I thought he was a girl, because of his eyes. Does he use mascara?" Vic was also drunk, but in the same quasi-lucid manner.

"No, he doesn't wear makeup. He just looks that way, naturally," I said, nuzzling the back of George's head.

"*I* have a cat," he said, showing a competitive side. "His name's Walter. He's deaf and completely white, but not albino. White cats are often deaf."

"I didn't know that."

"Yeah, some kind of genetic thing, and I named him after my uncle Walter, who was deaf. He's the sweetest little cat."

Then he smiled to himself, thinking of his Walter, but then he eyed George with what looked to me like a salacious gleam, and he reached across the table and petted him. "I also like dogs," he said. "I'm unusual that way. I like both. Cats and dogs."

"I like both, too. But it's not that unusual. At least according to Jung."

"Who's Young? The quarterback for the Niners? The lefty? Wasn't he Mormon?"

"No, Carl Jung, the psychoanalyst," I said, and I didn't bother mentioning that I had done psychoanalysis myself, for several years, but with a Freudian.

"Never heard of that Young," said Vic. "I never did therapy. But I should have. I *did* go to AA in the '80s after a DUI. But it didn't stick."

He smiled at that and lifted his shot glass, like a toast, and I lifted my glass in return, and we each took a sip of our drinks, silently toasting AA, like defiant drunks everywhere, and then George jumped off my lap and went onto Vic's lap, and I had to accept this. George has a promiscuous side, which wounds me, but I remind myself, in these moments, that I'm number one and that at the end of the day he'll be back with me, and I watched, without betraying any feelings, while Vic nuzzled and inhaled the back of George's head. "He's got a good smell to him," Vic said. "No anal funk."

"Of course there's no funk," I said, feeling defensive on George's behalf. "He keeps himself very clean. Licks himself all over. He's quite fastidious that way."

Vic nodded at this bit of information — he wasn't sure about my using the word "fastidious" — and finished his tequila. Then he said, "You a boxer, Lou?" He indicated my two black eyes from Diablo, the runoff from my broken nose.

"I used to be. In the Navy. A long time ago."

"Oh, yeah? Any good?"

"Not really. I was easy to hit but hard to put down. My chin was my jab."

Then for the hell of it and because I was drunk and feeling my ego, I pantomimed a sweet left hook to the body. Anyone who's ever boxed does that when they're drunk — throws punches, acts like they're Rocky Graziano — and I was also sending a message to Vic to not get too familiar with George, and Vic smiled, not perceiving the message. Then he called out to the bartender and ordered us two more tequilas and two Victoria beers. I made a motion for my wallet, but Vic said, "Forget about it. You're a vet. A Navy man. The booze is on me."

"Thank you. I appreciate it."

"How *did* you get those shiners and the busted nose?"

"Walked into a door."

"I've done that," he said. "I have a thing. I walk into glass doors. Can't tell you how many times it's happened. Mostly I bounce off because I'm skinny, but one time, I had a head of steam and walked right through, nearly cut off my left arm and died."

He extended his left arm then and showed me an ancient nasty scar that ran from his elbow to his armpit; it was on a pouch of skin hanging off the bone, what used to be his biceps. I said, "Must have hurt like hell."

"Not really. But there was a lot of blood, like a case of wine had been dropped."

Then the fresh drinks came, and we clinked and drank, and he said, "How long were you in the Navy, Lou?"

Vic was quite the conversationalist, but I really didn't mind. He was a sweet old thing, and George came back over to my lap, which helped, and I said, "Seven years. Eighty-seven to ninety-four, which included Desert Storm, but I was in the Pacific the whole time."

"What was your rank?"

"Warrant officer, master-at-arms."

"What's that?"

"Cop on a boat. Keep the boys in line. Did you ever serve?"

"No, 4-F for Vietnam. I have a hole in my ear from a mastoid operation gone wrong when I was a kid. You could put a straw in there" — he motioned to his ear — "and touch my brain."

"Really?" The booze had me gullible.

He laughed. "No! But there is a hole. Kept me out of the war, for which I am very grateful to this day."

We clinked our beers to that and had a couple more rounds, and I got the basic outline of Vic's story: born and raised in Reno, never left; a retired electrician and union man; a widower with no kids, just a cat; and he had been coming down to Baja, an area called the East Cape, to fish and drink, during the winter months, for the last thirty years. At the moment, he was in La Paz getting his truck fixed, which was why he was in the cantina, waiting and drinking.

All this to say that Vic and I took a shine to each other, and when he found out I played backgammon — somehow that came up — he begged me to come out to his place and play with him. He hadn't played in years, not since his wife died, and he had a hammock under a palapa where I could sleep, he said, and we could also go fishing, if I liked; he had a friend who would take us out the next day.

Well, this was one of those quick hothouse booze friendships — with my daddy issues throwing oil on the fire — and I accepted his invitation, and we made our plan. I'd collect my things, check out of my cheap hotel, and meet him at the garage in an hour, when his truck should be ready.

We had one more tequila to close the deal, and then I left the bar, a little wobbly, but I figured in an hour, I'd be sober enough to drive, and in the meantime the booze had me feeling ebullient, even hopeful about the future, *my* future. The day before, I had called the doctor from a Mexican burner phone, and he discreetly let me know that everything was all right back at the lodge, that our ruse had worked, which was welcome news: the Sinaloa wouldn't be looking for me and the Rosarito cops wouldn't be looking for me.

And on the internet, on the hotel computer, I had found a piece in the *LA Times* about the dead bodies in Joshua Tree. The police were assuming that it was a drug-related multiple homicide, but what made the story newsworthy was that one of the dead men, who had identification bearing the name Hoyt Marrow, was actually, according to fingerprints, a man named David Exel, wanted for a murder in Hollywood in 2005. Which seemed to be the main takeaway of the piece: a killer had finally been brought to some kind of justice, and this struck me as very promising: the cops wouldn't be looking too hard for anyone involved in such a case.

And as for Kunian and the Jalisco Cartel, I had no way of knowing if they were on to me, but I was walking around with a new mug and my trail was cold and strange. But, regardless, it was better to play it safe and keep moving, like going on this little adventure with Vic.

Plus, I had achieved my goal in coming to La Paz, which had been to mourn Ines, to find her shadow, and it happened on our third night there. I had left George in the hotel room — I was feeling a little mystical on tequila and morphine — and I went walking along the malecón, with its tourist cafés and restaurants overlooking the bay of La Paz.

And as I strolled, I kept seeing dark-haired women sitting at the café tables, and for a moment, I'd think it was Ines. I was trying to hallucinate her back to life, but it wasn't working. So I walked onto the beach, with the music and laughter from the cafés following me, and I sat down on the sand and looked out at the water, which was as black as the sky above.

Then I lay back and closed my fingers around some sand, pretending to hold Ines's hand, and I scoffed in my mind at my pathetic little game. But then suddenly I felt a delicate hand interlocking with mine, and I looked out of the corner of my eye, frightened, and it was Ines, right beside me. She looked as she did when I first met her years and years ago, and I was afraid to breathe, afraid to look at her fully and maybe scare her off.

So we just lay there, holding hands, and I said, in a whisper, "I love you, Ines," and this feeling, of her hand in mine, of her lying next to me, lasted for about ten minutes and then it was over. She had left as she had come, swiftly and unexpectedly, and that was my funeral for her.

2.

SO IT WAS TIME to leave La Paz, and back at my ugly, cheap hotel, which had a beautiful name, La Vida en Rosa, I drunkenly packed up, and when George and I stood in the doorway of our room, ready to leave, I thanked the room for having us, a ritual I maintain at hotels and motels when it's time to go, though I'm not sure why, but it feels rude and like bad luck if I don't do it.

We drove over to the garage near the cantina and Vic was ready to leave, but before we took off, the mechanic, seeing my Chevy, came right over to me and spoke to me through my open window. He had a big belly and thick black glasses, unusual on a mechanic, it seemed, and on the spot, he offered me three thousand American dollars for my Caprice. Car junkies really do love the '80s Caprice, and I thanked him but said no, and I followed Vic out of La Paz.

Vic's car was a red Toyota pickup, and once we were beyond the city limits, the whole southeast journey to the East Cape, about seventy miles, was on dirt roads, and it was gorgeous, stunning land we drove through. To the east was the Sea of Cortez, aquamarine and glistening like a bed of diamonds, and to the west was a semiarid plain of trees and cacti, with almost no development, just a few small ranches here and there.

After driving for about an hour, Vic led us onto the coastal road, a dangerous and narrow dirt trek on the edge of cliffs, with the ocean and death down below. I cursed the tequila in my system and hoped this wouldn't be the way George and I would die, though I recognized it might be karma for sending Diablo off a cliff.

Vic had told me that when I saw two large mounds on the plain we would be in his part of the East Cape, and that the mounds, which looked like whales, gave the area its unofficial name: Dos Ballenas. And when I saw the two whalelike formations, about ninety minutes into our journey, the light was beginning to change, dusk was coming on, and the sea, to my left, was now the color of mercury tinged with violet, and to the right, on the far horizon, were rolling mountains, also colored violet by the setting sun.

A few miles past the mounds, Vic turned off the coastal road onto another dirt road, heading west, and all around us, like all of the East Cape, was empty, untouched desert scrubland, with just a few small, isolated dwellings here and there, including a white yurt, which caught my eye.

Then, a quarter mile past the yurt, we turned onto an even more narrow dirt road, which cut through a grove of giant saguaro cacti, and this dirt road, it turned out, was Vic's driveway, because after about fifty yards it ended in a dusty clearing and we were at his house: a square cinder-block structure, painted blue. It was a very small house, and off to the side, on the right, was a thatched-roof palapa and a hammock.

We were really in the middle of nowhere, and when we got out of the cars, I stretched my legs and looked out at miles of gorgeous, unsullied land, which ended in the violet-hued mountains, and I wondered if this was what the Los Angeles Basin had looked like before it was developed and destroyed.

Then Vic asked, like a good host, "Do you need to take a crap? Because I don't have a toilet inside. Or should I say number two? That's what my wife called it. She had better manners."

"I think I'm all right," I said.

"Well, let me show you where the outhouse is anyway, in case you need it later."

He led us around to the back, where there was an old beat-up skiff and a bunch of saguaro cacti, two of which were used to hold up a laundry line. Twenty yards away, up a slight incline, was the outhouse, a narrow wooden shack with a crescent moon cut into the door.

"Good not to have it too close," Vic said, pointing at the thing, "but there's a bag of lye in there with a scoop; just don't get it in your eyes. And you can piss anywhere you like. The outhouse is just for craps and number two, whatever you want to call it."

"Good to know," I said.

"I thought of putting in a toilet when I built this place thirty years ago, but even then septic tanks cost a lot, and commodes, you know, waste a lot of water, and you've got to be careful out here with water. *Very* careful."

Vic then explained to me that there was no running water or electricity in Dos Ballenas, no infrastructure whatsoever in its thirty or so square miles, and so his house had a water tank and solar panels on the roof, with a gas generator as backup.

After that little speech, he pointed out the shower, which was a spigot and valve poking out of the house's back wall, with a concrete base to stand on. "The shower only has cold water," he said, "but even then, it's a luxury. Showers use a lot of water. *A lot.* Even more than toilets. So once a week, maybe twice if I'm gamey, but that's it for bathing. Which is also when I do laundry. I walk on my shirts and underwear, like a rinse cycle."

Done now with the tour, we went back around to the front. Vic unlocked the front door, and I was immediately hit with a blast of pungent old-man sweat, like the house was a gigantic extension and expression of Vic's armpits, which made sense considering the shower restrictions.

But despite the odor, which was like a combination of urine and vinegar, Vic's place, just one large, square room, was pleasant to be in: it was neat and sparsely furnished, had good feng shui. There were windows at the front and back, which Vic opened for cross ventilation, and then he turned on a ceiling fan, which moved the sweaty smell around nicely.

That accomplished, he asked if I wanted a Victoria beer, and I said sure, and he went into the kitchen area, which was composed of a small two-burner stove, a sink, a half size fridge, and a wooden table for two.

I followed him to the fridge and gave the rest of the place a closer scan: across from the kitchen area was the "living room" — a couch, two old reclining chairs, a couple of lamps, and a bookshelf of warped paperback novels, mostly bodice rippers, remnants perhaps of Vic's dead wife.

At the far end of the room, in the left-hand corner, was Vic's queen-size bed, which sagged in the middle, and across from the bed was a stand-alone wooden closet and a wooden dresser, both painted eggshell blue. The floor was Mexican tile, which made the room cool, and while Vic opened the beers, George was running around the place, sniffing everywhere, which was when Walter, Vic's cat, rather elegant and completely white as advertised, emerged from beneath Vic's bed, and George raced over to him, in attack mode, but then skidded to a stop.

Maybe because he was deaf, Walter had an eerie Zen calm about him, which spoke to George on some deep level, and he and the white cat just stared at each other.

Normally, though, George would have tried to kill Walter, which I had forgotten to mention to Vic, having forgotten that he had a cat, and I was about to go grab George, but then Walter, stretching his legs rather languorously, strolled right past George, as if he wasn't there, and George trailed after him, meekly, while secretly trying to get his nose into Walter's anus. Which Walter didn't seem to mind at all, and, in fact, he looked at George over his shoulder, like a woman in an Italian movie from the '50s, and I could see why George was enamored.

Then Walter, displaying his whimsical cat nature, suddenly raced out the open front door.

George was slow off the mark but after a moment's hesitation, he was after him, like a young lover, and Vic said, watching this interplay, "For some reason dogs go crazy for Walter."

"Yeah, I've never seen George behave like that with a cat."

We took our beers outside and sat under the open-air palapa in camp chairs, looking out at the desert plain and the purple mountains. We clinked our bottles and drank up.

Meanwhile, George was following Walter around the dusty yard, getting a tour, and they made a handsome couple: George, with his sleek tan suit and bedroom eyes, and Walter, as white as a bridal gown and sculpted like a totem on a pharaoh's grave.

Vic said, "You smoke marijuana, Lou?"

"Daily," I said, and Vic smiled and went back into the house.

He returned with a tobacco pouch filled with weed and tobacco and rolled us a wonderful spliff. So we drank our beers and smoked, and, as the sun set, the Baja air was soft and warm, perfect for being stuck in a human body.

It was all a small taste of heaven, and for a little while, I could let go that I had recently killed a man and had swapped out my face for my father's. And I could also let go, for a minute, this feeling that something or someone was coming for me. Though I knew, deep down, that it *would* happen; it had to. *You can run but you can't hide* is one of those immutable laws of life, like impermanence or karma or death.

But that night I was safe, and, eventually, Vic broke out the board and we had a delightful evening of beer, weed, and backgammon, punctuated by a dinner of scrambled eggs and fried onions, which was one of the best meals I'd ever had. I guess I was in a good mood.

Around midnight, the party was winding down — Vic, after vomiting, had passed out on his bed — so I took a morphine pill, and George and I went out to the hammock, with three Mexican blankets and a pillow that Vic had laid out earlier.

I placed one of the blankets over the mesh, like a sheet, so George's paws wouldn't get stuck. Then we got into the hammock, and with George under the blankets, like a hot-water bottle by my side, I lay on my back and looked up at the sky, which was populated with hundreds if not thousands of stars. There was no light pollution in the East Cape — the whole wheeling galaxy was visible — and I felt like a very lucky man.

Then the morphine did its thing, and the galaxy was snuffed out like a candle.

What followed was mostly a dreamless night, except for one nightmare in which the soles of my feet peeled open, like they'd been slit with a knife, and I watched in horror as white maggot eggs, the size of marbles, rolled out of my feet and became worms.

* * *

In the morning, Vic and I were at his little kitchen table, drinking black coffee and nursing our hangovers. We weren't verbal yet, but the backgammon board was out, and we were already setting up the pieces, which are called pips, and like mirrors to each other, Walter was in Vic's lap and George was in mine.

Despite being booze sick, we were both eager to play again because we were evenly matched, which isn't so easy to find in backgammon — most people don't know what they're doing — and so we liked playing each other, it was addictive, and once we got the board arranged, I was all set to throw the dice and kick off a new game, but then Vic got a call on his cell phone, which surprised me. But clearly there was cell reception in Dos Ballenas — later I would find out why — and Vic answered his battered Android device and put it on speakerphone, miming to me that it was the only way he could hear whoever was talking.

I made a motion to stand up and give him privacy, but Vic waved at me to sit down, and so I listened in on the call, which maybe I shouldn't have. The gist of what I heard was that his sister, in a nursing home in Seattle, was very sick and might pass in the next twenty-four hours, and when Vic hung up, he looked stricken.

Then he said, "Could you take me to the airport in del Cabo, Lou? I don't think I can drive myself there — I'm all shook up — but I gotta go see her and say goodbye. She's the only family I have left and...and you could stay here. Look after Walter. And the waterman is coming in two days. I have to pay or I won't have water when I come back. I'll give you the money."

I readily agreed to this — I wanted to help Vic — and after he got the call, I took him to the airport in San José del Cabo, a ninety-minute drive to the south, and Vic went straightaway to see his sister, who was older and had half raised him. This was the middle of February 2020, and at first, Vic's sister hung on, but then two weeks after he got there, she died of COVID, and then he got it and died — the pandemic had begun — and I ended up squatting in Vic's house for the next three years, and he never even knew my real name.

3.

IT STARTED OUT AS a good place to be during a plague, while also being on the run, an interesting combination, but then as time went on, I just didn't want to leave. I had it too good. I swam every day. I fished. I snorkeled. I smoked weed. I ate weed. I stopped eating meat. I didn't kill anybody. I resumed my Buddhist studies.

All of which I needed.

Especially the Buddhism.

I had gotten in a bad way in the months and years leading up to the pandemic, and I needed to change. Diablo was the eighth man I had killed, and it was always in self-defense, in situations in which I could have also been killed, but each time I had done it I had felt the sickening pull of the abyss, of becoming a shadow human, impervious to the suffering of others.

So, of course, I never wanted to kill again — I feared becoming a monster — but we all have these behaviors we wish to stop but can't. They are merry-go-rounds of hell of our own making, repetitious patterns of suffering, and the Buddhists call this cycle of pain "samsara." It's like being an actor and choosing to play the same scene again and again and again...

Take me, for example. My father beat me, and so what did I do? I went out into life and found my father in all sorts of disguises, and eight times, I did what I couldn't do as a child but must have wished for. I killed the bad man. Maybe I thought that was a way to make the scene better, but it only made it worse.

So, not to be grandiose, but I figured I had just about the most horrible samsara there is: I kept killing other human beings. But the Buddha knew how to deal with this, even a real bad case like mine. His whole mission in life was to teach people how to break the cycles of samsara, and so I just had to follow his instructions, some of which were over my head, but his first teaching, the Four Noble Truths, is broken down into four simple steps (my interpretation) that even I could follow:

1. **Acknowledge that you suffer.** Life is difficult, and we are often afraid and confused, in part because everything is impermanent and always changing. So we have no control. Over anything. Except for our own behavior, and that's exceedingly dicey until we get to noble truths two through four. Also, making things even harder is the fact that we will die and don't know when. On top of that, everyone we know and love will also die! (Including George! Including Walter! It can't be!) So all this causes tremendous pain and suffering, which we inevitably make worse.

2. **Analyze and study your suffering.** Come to understand that impermanence is the way things are, no getting around it, and so try not to fight it. This too shall pass, and all that. The good things and the bad things. But because all this uncertainty makes us terribly anxious, we run like crazy from ourselves and from our pain and can barely tolerate being in our own skin. Therefore, study all the neurotic ways in which you run from yourself and come to understand that all this running *makes things worse, much worse!* So identify your crazy behaviors and distorted thinking and take responsibility for it all. Which means: don't blame others! It's a waste of time. And anyone you blame is actually your greatest teacher. They show you where you need to grow.

3. **Having studied your pain, begin to behave yourself!** Stop doing all these neurotic things, all this acting out; stop all this running from pain — the constant pursuit of distraction and the constant pursuit of pleasure, which is often pain in disguise — and you'll notice that you feel better, that you are suffering less. You can even glimpse peace! And because you're suffering less and not shooting yourself in the foot so much, you can help others to suffer less. And this is very important: helping others. It's why we're here. Just about. Also, it's worth repeating: refrain from your bad habits and behave yourself! If you don't refrain and you don't behave, you can't get off the samsaric merry-go-round of suffering and causing others to suffer. But if you do misbehave, show yourself compassion and try again. And this applies to so many things we do samsarically: lying, drinking too much, eating too much, chasing after praise, putting ourselves down, slandering others, playing the victim, holding grudges, lashing out in anger, giving over to lust, always having to be right, wallowing in self-pity . . . all the above and so much more! But we can learn to refrain from these things, especially if we recognize the negative karma we create, the cause and effect of our behaviors. If you act like a jerk, you will suffer! If you play the victim, you will suffer! If you don't let go of your looping thinking, you will suffer! So break the patterns and glimpse liberation! That's good karma! And kindness, compassion, generosity, and mindfulness are our tools to achieve this! So use them! And don't forget, most importantly: practice meditation! It's good for you! You will become more aware of your thinking, of the chattering, often quite negative voice inside your head, and you will learn to work with all that internal babble. The Buddha said, "The mind is everything. What you think, you become."

4. **Because you've stopped acting out (in my case, killing people) or have begun to lessen your acting out and have glimpsed**

a bit of peace as a result, repeat steps one through three like your life depends on it, because it does, and if you really apply yourself, which the Buddha's second teaching, the Noble Eightfold Path, can also help you with, you might actually attain enlightenment, also known as nirvana. And nirvana is achieved by liberating yourself from samsara. Which means you need samsara, just like the lotus flower needs mud to grow, and nirvana, if you manage to get there, is a place of profound equanimity, empty of conflict, because it's also empty of labels and words, like mud and flower, samsara and nirvana, *you* and *me*. There is no division, it turns out, everything is one, and when we quiet ourselves, we can perceive this, even if only for a moment, because we're actually already enlightened! In fact, we've been enlightened this whole damn time and nirvana is like an all-night diner. It's always open. You can always go there. All of which is a big teaching: we come equipped from the start with everything we need to look deep into our own mind and the mind of the world, but how do we learn to see? From our suffering. Which is our gold. Our fortune. Our mud. The Buddha said, in part, "I teach only suffering and the transformation of suffering." And this learning from suffering is the dharma, the truth, the way, which is to take our pain and turn it into love and compassion, for ourselves and others, and the more we do this, the more we wake up and notice how beautiful everything is, how all of life is one, and that's what Buddhism means: to wake up.

So for three years in Dos Ballenas, living monkishly, except for my ménage with George and Walter, that's what I was desperately trying to do: wake up!

And applying steps two and three, I identified that I had to stop killing people, and the practical way to help achieve this was to stop putting myself in the position where this would happen, which was living in Los

Angeles and being a private investigator. I had thought my goal, when I got my new face, was to be able to return to my life, but as the COVID years passed, I didn't want to go back, and the truth is, I was afraid to go back. I was afraid that I would revert.

Now, when you work on yourself in Buddhism, the goal is to be able to help others, to get in the mix and do some good, but I figured it might be enough for the rest of my life just not to kill again, though I was certainly fine with being kind to anyone whose path I might cross. I could definitely do that. And in Dos Ballenas, it was easy. There weren't that many people around to be kind to, which also meant there was much less chance of killing anyone.

And so, like I said, it seemed like the best thing I could do for the planet and other human beings was to just lie low and be very quiet, not cause any more suffering, and be what they called in Buddhism a "solitary realizer," a Prateyaka Buddha, as opposed to a bodhisattva, who gets in the trenches of life and tries to help anybody they can.

*   *   *

So it was a contemplative time to say the least, and I didn't have television or the internet to distract me. Once a month, though, on supply runs, I did go into civilization, to La Paz or San José del Cabo, and using hotel business centers, I would get on a computer to take care of a few things back in LA, and, invariably, I'd get a small dose of the world's clamor and its internet poison, but nothing like the daily dosage of internet hell that most people absorb and that I used to take in, and this lessening of web consumption was very freeing.

But it's not like I became numb to the hideous troubles of the world. It's just that I wasn't as consumed by and as addicted to them as I had been in the past, and this helped create space in my mind to study the dharma, but what also liberated me to do this work was that after a while I stopped worrying that anyone was coming for me. Too much time had passed. *And I* wasn't that important. Another Buddhist lesson.

But it wasn't just a period of spiritual growth: I was also transforming physically. Swimming in the ocean every day for three years, I became incredibly lean and strong. In fact, I had never felt more powerful or vital, not even as a young man, and with the sun and saltwater curing it, my father's face, as the years passed, morphed as well, until it became my own face, like a fresh coin with a new president on it.

Practically speaking, though, I couldn't stay in Mexico working on myself forever. Money was becoming a problem. I had started off — after paying the doctor — with the thirty-five K stolen from Kunian's boat, plus eight thousand dollars in my Chase account in LA, but by January 2023, my third year in seclusion, I was running out of funds.

It was, of course, incredibly cheap to squat at Vic's: water and other living expenses cost me about four thousand a year, helped by the fact that most of our food, protein at least, I got from the sea. But the problem was back in LA. I owned a run-down four-room bungalow in Beachwood Canyon, which had been willed to me by an elderly client, and while I had no mortgage to pay, the taxes and quasi-paused utilities came to about eleven thousand a year, which meant that by January, when everything went to hell again, I was down to about a thousand bucks. I had stopped the bleeding, somewhat, in the spring of 2022, by selling my Caprice to that mechanic in La Paz, a nice man named Felix, for what he had first offered me, three thousand American dollars, but now, at the beginning of 2023, I was just about out and was really going to have to leave my little Buddhist cocoon.

What I needed to do — and I had known this for months — was go up to LA in Vic's truck and sell my house. In the LA market, even my little bungalow would fetch eight or nine hundred grand, maybe even a million. Then I could come back down and live off that in Dos Ballenas for the rest of my natural life, not hurting anyone and continuing my studies, while literally burying my head in the sand at the beach, as the world played out its collective samsara of self-destruction, hate, and greed. As a cop and a private cop, I had been part of the fight against the entropy, standing up for the little guy, or so I thought, but in the end, I had done more harm than good, and so the thing to do was get up to LA, sell my house, and retire permanently. It was a coward's plan to quit the world, but at least it was a plan.

Except I kept delaying taking any sort of action, in part because I hadn't kept up with the bureaucratic necessities that go along with being on the run. An American can wander around Mexico for six months without papers of any kind, but I had been in the country for three years! Also, my passport and driver's license had both expired, and what it all added up to was that at the border, if I tried to cross, the Mexicans were going to fine me substantially, maybe even detain me, and the Americans wouldn't let me in, anyway.

To avoid this, I needed to write letters to government agencies and make phone calls and fill out internet forms. I also needed a mailing address, but there was no postal service in Dos Ballenas. All of this, naturally, could be figured out and done, but I kept procrastinating endlessly; my ability to function in the world felt atrophied after so many years of near isolation.

So I kept doing nothing, like a child who won't clean their room.

But I was in denial. Soon my money would run out.

4.

MY LAST DAY SQUATTING at Vic's, though I didn't know it then, was Friday, January 20, 2023, and while it ended violently, it began peacefully, as I followed my usual routine.

I was up at five, had a coffee, a joint, and two hard-boiled eggs with salt.

Then, in the predawn light, I jogged down the driveway to the east-west dirt road.

It was chilly out, high fifties, and I was wearing my bathing suit (a pair of khaki pants I had cut off at mid-thigh), a T-shirt, a ratty old sweater, and sneakers. Clouds obscured the stars and the moon, but there was enough light to see by, and I was all alone in the empty desert world, with its magnificent silence: no sounds of man, no hum of machinery.

A few minutes into my run, I jogged past Kathy and Zim's yurt, which glowed white in the predawn. Kathy and Zim, both in their early seventies, were old pot growers from Humboldt County and had been coming down to the East Cape since the '70s. They were the closest thing I had to friends — they were my weed suppliers — and a mile after I passed their yurt, I hit the coastal dirt road and the cliff line, and straight ahead was the ocean, vast and monstrous. The sea at night has always felt menacing to me, even though I was in the Navy for years. I turned right on the cliff road, jogging at a nice clip, and after two hundred yards, the road dipped down to an old arroyo and then rose again steeply.

It was here, at the mouth of the arroyo, that one could gain entry to the beach, and just in from the dirt road was where Dan lived with his wife, Yuko. They were also in their early seventies, and I guess you could say they were my other two friends in Dos Ballenas, but we weren't that close, because I was, more or less, Dan's employee. Also, he was surly as hell, and Yuko was very private, though once a month, she would cut my hair and gently touch my shoulders, which was my only human contact for years.

That winter, Dan and Yuko had been living on the beach since mid-November, having come down from Tacoma in their old Lance Camper, which they parked right on the sand, ten yards from the road and thirty yards from the water. But they didn't sleep in the camper. They slept in a big tent and had chairs around a firepit, where they did their cooking.

People could live and camp on the beach in Dos Ballenas — there was no government presence — and most of the camper tourists were transient, would stay just a week or two, but Dan and Yuko nested there every year for about five months total and had been coming to that exact spot for decades. Up in Tacoma, Dan still made a living as a commercial fisherman, but from November to March, he and Yuko lived off the sea in Dos Ballenas.

They had a ten-foot metal skiff, which they towed behind the camper, and it used to be their son and then grandson who would go out fishing with Dan, because to get the skiff in the ocean and past the first break, you needed two people. But their grandson got married in 2019 and wasn't coming down to Mexico anymore, and so I became Dan's first mate my first winter there and the next two that followed, and my payment was in fish.

Luckily, Dan wasn't a talkative guy, which made spending time with him in a boat easy to take, and he liked to be in the water between 5:30 and 5:45, as the sun was rising. Monday, Wednesday, Friday was our usual schedule, and we'd fish till nine or ten, before it got too hot.

It was a good routine, and we'd catch enough in those three days to feed Dan, Yuko, George, me, and Walter for the whole week, with some extra to share or trade, like I traded fish for weed from Kathy and Zim, and traded fish for eggs from the local Mexican families, who lived in small ranches to the west, at the base of the mountains.

Anyway, that morning, when I arrived at the campsite, Dan grunted hello, which was a lot from him. He was barefoot, in a bathing suit and cardigan sweater, and he was sitting in a camp chair by the firepit, sipping a coffee.

Yuko was still asleep in their tent, and the firelight dramatized Dan's stoic features: his face was seamed from years of sun exposure, and he had a long, bony nose, like a heron, which was probably why fishing was his vocation.

As I took off my sneakers, he stood up — he was tall, with ropy muscles — and threw the rest of his coffee in the fire. He was always anxious to get going in the morning, and if I was a few minutes late, he didn't like it and would let me know, but that morning, thankfully, I was on time, and once my sneakers were off, he went immediately to the front of the ten-foot metal skiff, and I went to the stern.

I threw my T-shirt and sweater into the boat — all the fishing gear was already in there — and then Dan, with his back to me, reached behind himself, got his hands on the edge of the boat, and, together, we lifted the metal skiff.

We then had to carry it the thirty yards to the water, which wasn't easy, but Dan, even in his seventies, was still incredibly strong from years of working outdoors, and his hands were noticeably powerful, covered as they were with thick veins, like a tangle of bait worms.

As we carried the boat across the sand, the light was rapidly changing — from purple to light purple to pink — and we had to stop every ten yards or so because the metal skiff, with its oars and its outboard motor, was quite heavy, and walking in the sand made it even heavier.

But then we got the boat into the cold water, which was gunmetal gray melting into violet. The morning light was playing with the sea, like it was mixing paints, and we waded the skiff out to where the violet-colored water was about three feet deep.

Then Dan climbed in, sat on the middle bench, facing me, and readied the oars.

On the horizon, the sun was beginning to emerge from the sea, a fiery crescent, and I stood behind the boat, waiting for a big wave to break and rush past us, and as it did, Dan shouted, "Now!"

Which was when I began to push the boat as hard as I could — my legs churning in the shallow water — while Dan was working the oars like crazy, fighting the current.

We had to get the boat through the first break before it crashed on him or flipped the boat backwards if we didn't time it right, and when the water suddenly became deep, I started swimming behind the boat, pushing it the best I could, and, like every morning, we made it just in time, and Dan and the boat rose and crested the tall wave right before it crashed, though then it crashed on me, as it always did, but I ducked under it, while Dan kept rowing to be well clear of the next breaker.

When I came up for air, I swam after him and clambered on board, pushing myself up on the edge of the skiff. I banged my legs as I did most mornings — I had notches up and down my shin bones — but then I was in the boat, and Dan, who had shifted over to the back bench, threw me a towel, which I wrapped around my shoulders. Then he lowered the large propeller and yanked the cord, viciously, and nothing happened. But on the second pull, the motor coughed awake, and we set off, moving fast right away, up and down the swells. I was on the middle bench, facing forward, and there were long sun candles across the surface of the sea, golden pathways to the edge of the world.

Then I looked back at the beach for a moment and an enormous half-moon was now visible, setting behind the mountains to the west, like a giant sleepy eye, and perhaps having a premonition, I wondered if it was an evil eye.

* * *

We caught a tuna and a dorado, and, luckily, they were both males, because it was an unwritten rule that the females, with their thousands of precious eggs, had to be thrown back. The Sea of Cortez was still quite vital and full of life, but Dan had told me that in the last forty years, the stock of fish had dropped at least 30 percent.

Around ten a.m., we headed back, and I jumped out fifty yards from shore and swam and bodysurfed my way in. This way Dan could manage the boat with less weight, which made it easier for him, and it was always so impressive the way he guided that metal boat to shore.

That day the waves were especially big, four or five feet, and for a moment the skiff hovered on the lip of the giant wave that Dan had chosen for passage, and the boat was sticking straight out of the water, aimed at the shore like a missile.

Then, with Dan in the back, using one of the oars like a rudder, the skiff suddenly came shooting down the face of the wave, going much too fast, barely ahead of the curling tunnel, but Dan and the boat outraced it and were carried all the way in, the skiff coming to a stop in the wet shoreline sand.

I caught the tail end of the same wave and bodysurfed in, and Dan, accustomed to his own heroics, stepped out of the boat like a Viking, and we carried it back across the sand, our last exertion of the day.

At the campsite, I sat in a beach chair and sipped a beer and watched Yuko clean the fish at a portable table. The sun, over the years, had baked her a dark brown, and she had a long, beautiful braid of iron-gray hair that went to the middle of her back. She was naked under a simple cotton housedress — the sunlight made the thin fabric translucent — and I thought about her cutting my hair.

When she was done cleaning the fish, I took my share home, wrapped in paper, and George, Walter, and I had some of the raw tuna for our late morning breakfast — I guess you could call it sashimi. After we ate, we all got into bed, Vic's old bed, for our siesta.

Walter started off by sitting on my chest and drooling on me, a sign of feline affection, I've been told. Then he positioned himself above my head on the pillow, and George, under the meager blanket, snuggled in next to my torso, our usual threesome arrangement, and I let out a childlike giggle of pure happiness, which harkened back to some childhood I never even had.

Then, after a little more shifting about, we all sighed at the same time, our breaths slowing in unison as we fell asleep.

* * *

After our nap, I ate a marijuana cookie — part of my trade agreement with Kathy and Zim — and walked to the beach to go snorkeling, which would prove to be my undoing.

My favorite diving spot was a quarter mile up the sand from Dan and Yuko's camp and was marked by two things: (1) on the cliff above there was a modern glass house, and (2) out in the water, about a hundred yards, were enormous boulders, arranged, by chance, like a wall, and this wall created a wide swath of water that was nearly calm, with the rocks dissipating the big waves. Which made the snorkeling here fantastic. The calmer water had excellent visibility — no churn — and what made this spot, this natural harbor, truly special was a sunken fishing boat. It was a trawler about forty feet long, which had hit the rocks twenty years ago during a storm and sunk, and thousands of fish now used it like a coral reef.

That day, as I began to feel the cookie, I swam out and started diving down by the boat, watching the schools of silvery fish swim in and out of the broken vessel and through shafts of sunlight from the world above. It was all so beautiful. The doomed boat, to me, was as mysterious as the *Titanic,* and some days, when I was out there, an octopus would emerge from inside the hull and look at me with very sad eyes — how could it not be sad with a brain that big? — but I didn't see the octopus that day, and as for humans, I was all alone.

Almost no one in Dos Ballenas, which had a population of about fifty souls, liked to snorkel, which was great for me — I had the snorkeling spot all to myself — and these non-snorkelers I had divided into three categories: the Mexican ranch families, to the west, at the base of the mountains;

the retired working-class American expats on the plain; and the eight wealthy families, from various countries, who owned the cliff houses that overlooked the water and the miles of empty, pristine beach.

Vic had been part of the expat plain dwellers, old contractors and tradesfolk, most of them from the Pacific Northwest, with a few from Nevada. These people lived in squat concrete boxes or old trailers or house-like palapas, all on tiny parcels of land they had purchased for next to nothing back in the '80s and early '90s. There were also, on the plain, a few old hippie types, like Kathy and Zim.

The wealthy class of Dos Ballenas was the eight families on the cliffs, and they lived in beautiful white houses, Spanish stucco or modern sleek, and these cliff houses were rigged with expensive solar-powered systems, large water tanks, and powerful backup generators.

About a mile separated each cliff house from its neighbors, which gave them plenty of privacy, and they all had long staircases down to the sand and the water, to basically their own private beach. The house by the snorkeling spot, for example, had concrete steps, painted white and built zigzag fashion into the scrubby cliffside, climbing up about a hundred feet.

But you couldn't see this house from the beach; it was set too far back from the cliff edge, though I had seen it while out fishing with Dan. It was one of the modern houses, and it had two stories, like two big glass boxes, one piled on top of the other.

The second-floor box had an enormous balcony, which must have had incredible views, and the ground-floor box opened onto a large infinity swimming pool that was surrounded by white lounges. The whole place looked amazing from the sea, and the other houses on the cliffs were all owned by families who would make an appearance at some point during the year, but this was the one house where the owner never showed up.

The only people who stayed there were renters, though not that often. Every six weeks or so, the house would be occupied, usually just for a few days, and none of the local expats even knew who owned the place, which had been built in the last five years and was sometimes called the Rock House, because of the rocks out in the water in front of it, *and* because Mick Jagger had supposedly stayed there once, though nobody had actually seen him.

The people who did stay there would arrive in expensive tinted-window SUVs, part of the package with the house, it seemed. They would be driven in from San José del Cabo or La Paz, and sometimes the renters ventured down to the water to swim, but it was surprising how infrequently they took advantage of the empty beach; they preferred to stay up by the pool, looking out at the sea, which in many ways made sense. There were sharks out in the water — not any more than in most places, but you don't need many — and the nearest hospitals were ninety minutes away.

When the renters did come down to the beach, they were often very beautiful people: young women with legs that started at their shoulders, and men who looked like tennis stars a few years past their prime. These renters were mostly rich South Americans or Europeans, though sometimes wealthy Americans stayed there as well.

When I was out in Dan's boat, it did look very glamorous around that pool, and sometimes I had wished, during my three years in Dos Ballenas, that I would get invited up there, just to see what it was like, but of course it had never happened. No one from the Rock House had ever even spoken to me, probably because I had something of a feral look going on. Three years in the sun had turned me a cancerous dark brown, like I had been shipwrecked, and I often had a thick black and silver beard, which I would hack off every three months or so.

That day, I was at a peak of beard growth, and I was doing my usual thing, just snorkeling about, stoned on my cookie, and when I would dive down to get a closer look at the ruins of the boat, I could hear the underwater cries of the gray whales.

November to March was when they would arrive from the cold northern Pacific to mate and have babies in the warm, bulblike dead end of the Sea of Cortez, and often the whales would pass Dan and me in our little boat, swimming north, like up a tube, behaving like salmon or, more lewdly, sperm, and if you look at it on a map, the shape of the Sea of Cortez does look cervical. But nothing surprising in that. Nature repeats itself, as we all know, in the miniature and the macro.

Anyway, after about an hour of snorkeling, I did one final dive, and when I resurfaced and lifted my head out of the water, to orient myself to the shore, I saw a woman on the beach, sitting on a towel. One of the beautiful people from the Rock House had ventured down.

* * *

As I emerged from the water, carrying my fins, she stood up from her towel, which was right next to where I had left my towel and gear bag.

"Hola," she said brightly, with a non-Spanish accent.

Then she added, haltingly, "¿Como estuvo el snorkeling?"

She was smiling and very pretty, with an elegant unpainted mouth, a small, fine nose, and large blue eyes that seemed both innocent and intelligent, which would match the age I placed her at: late twenties or early thirties, someone not yet broken by life, but also no longer a child. She was on the small side, maybe five four, and her hair was sandy blonde, pulled back tightly from her forehead with a white band. There were charming freckles across her cheeks and the bridge of her nose, but she was mostly quite pale, and I didn't want to let my eyes drop, but I could see, peripherally, that she was wearing a flimsy white bikini and that she had a lovely, discreet figure, not bursting at the seams, but not malnourished, either.

"I speak English," I said.

"You're American? I'm shocked," she said, rather confidently. Her accent was English, maybe working-class, I thought, but it was hard for me to tell. All English accents, to my provincial ears, sound quite sophisticated.

"Yes, I'm American...but I...I live here."

"You look—I didn't think you were American. Well, how was the snorkeling?"

"Very beautiful," I said, and I was finding it hard to get the words out. I hadn't spoken to a young woman — or a young person for that matter — in a very long time. In my social set of septuagenarians, I had gotten used to being the baby of the group.

"I bet it was beautiful," she said, and then she picked up a large mesh bag from her towel, and inside it, I could see fins, a mask, and a snorkel. She took out the mask, seemingly to prove a point, and said, "Do you think you could take me? I've watched you the last few days from up there." She pointed at the cliff. "And today is my last day. My last chance."

She was very forward, but also somehow polite. Maybe it was the English accent. But before I could say anything, she said, "Just for ten minutes? I've never actually been snorkeling, and I've been stuck up there wondering what it's like."

She looked at me pleadingly, and it felt impossible to say no. I mumbled, "I guess I could keep an eye on you..."

"I should tell you I'm not a very good swimmer. But there's a life vest in here. I found all this stuff up at the house."

She then pulled a white vest out of the bag and held it out to me, as proof.

This alarmed me. I said, "If you're not a good swimmer, I don't know if we should —"

"I promise I won't drown. I've been practicing in the pool. With the mask and the snorkel, *and* the fins."

I looked away, uncertain, stoned, and confused. A beautiful young woman, who couldn't swim well, wanted me to take her snorkeling, and it was like my brain had no reference point for such things. I had spent most of the last three years reading the Dalai Lama and conversing one-sidedly with George and Walter in a gibberish kind of baby talk, full of my declarations of love, and so I felt wholly unprepared for the current situation. I went into a bit of a fugue state, and the girl jumped in. "I'm sorry to be all over you like this. It's so rude. My name's Frances."

She reached out her hand, rather proudly, and we shook. It was the first woman's hand I had held since the apparition of Ines on the beach in La Paz, and I told her my name was Lou. I was very used to the lie at this point, but it had also become a kind of truth, like it was a new name to go with a new face.

"So do you think you could take me?" she asked. "I'm sorry to be pushy."

I wanted to take her — it seemed so important to her — but it also felt like a foolish thing to do: she had said she wasn't a good swimmer, and so I tried to get out of it. I gestured to the cliff. "There's nobody up there who can go with you?"

She looked away, like I had said something painful, and then she said, "No. No one up there…Listen, I understand. I'm being so pushy. I just…Well, it's nice to meet you."

She offered me her hand again, awkwardly. She was all confused and young, and we shook again, and I said, wanting to please her, "You really want to snorkel?"

"Yes, very much," she said, smiling brightly.

"Okay. We'll go for ten minutes. And put the vest on."

She did this right away, zipping it up, and I figured with the vest there was no chance she could drown and so the risk wasn't too great. We then walked down to the water's edge, and I showed her how to prepare her mask, with a bit of saliva and saltwater, to keep it from fogging up. Then we put our fins on, and I said, "We walk in backwards. It's easier."

"Okay," she said, and we took two steps, but then she stopped. "Are there sharks out there?"

I hesitated, then said, "Yes, but they don't usually come in this close and almost never this time of day."

"What time of day *do* they come in?"

"Like I said, they usually don't come in this close, but if they did, they only feed very early in the morning or at night. I've been snorkeling here for three years, and I've never seen a shark this time of day."

Which wasn't entirely true; I had occasionally seen sand sharks, which scared the shit out of me every time, but they weren't man-eaters, and they would only bite if provoked, and I didn't provoke. I'd hightail it back to shore and not snorkel for a week to appease the gods and build my courage back up. "So don't worry," I added. "The chances of getting bit by a shark are almost like being in a plane crash."

"All right," she said, a little meekly — my plane crash reference wasn't the most reassuring — and we started stepping backwards into the water.

When it was deep enough, we turned around and I said, "We'll swim out about thirty, forty yards, and when you look down, you'll see a sunken ship and lots of fish. Okay?"

She nodded, and I could see, even behind her snorkeling mask, that she was quite scared. I said, "Are you sure you want to do this?"

"Yes," she said, and to show me how brave she was, she put her snorkel in her mouth and started doggy-paddling, with her head out of the water. It was effective enough, not quite a proper crawl, and I paddled alongside her.

When we were out about forty yards, I said, "Look down and you'll see fish. The water is very clear."

But instead of looking down, she looked back at the beach, spat the snorkel out, and said, "I didn't realize we were out so far. Oh, my God!"

She looked on the verge of panicking, and if she hadn't had the life vest buoying her, she might have started drowning, and then she *did* start drowning. She threw her arms around my neck, squeezing me tight, and tried to push me down under the water, which is the common reaction of a drowning person: to attack anyone within range, including the person who could help them. Luckily, she was a small thing, and I was able to detach her. Treading water, I held her at arm's length and said firmly, "You have to calm down, Frances!"

It took a moment, but then I saw the panic go out of her eyes and she realized she was okay, that the vest would keep her afloat, and that she was somewhere beautiful: in the warm blue-green sea, looking at the magnificent empty beach and the cliffs from a perspective she had never experienced before. And a calm came over her, and she even smiled.

She said, "I'm sorry...I..."

"It's okay," I said, letting go of her. "Just take one look below, don't worry about using the snorkel, and then we'll swim back."

"All right," she said. "Can you hold my hand?"

"Yes," I said, and I took her lovely, delicate hand — what had I gotten into? — and she lowered her mask into the water. After twenty seconds, she lifted her face out and said, "God, it's so beautiful! I'm not ready to go back. Is that okay?"

I was a little nervous but said, "All right. You seem better now."

Smiling behind her mask, she put her face back down in the water, and for the next ten minutes, we hovered about, holding hands, as she spied on a world she had never seen before. Then, breathless, she said, bringing her face out of the water, "I'm ready to go back."

I said, "One last thing, since we're out here. Put your whole head under water and see if you can hear the whales."

"Really? We've been watching them from up there, but I didn't know you could actually hear them."

"Yes, you can hear them. It's beautiful. Very plaintive."

She cocked her head at me. I think she was impressed by my vocabulary, and then she bravely ducked her whole head under the water, and when she reemerged, she said, "Does it sound like high-pitched whistles?"

"Yes. Or coyotes under water. That's what it sounds like to me."

She ducked back under and listened some more, and then we swam in.

When we got back to the towels, she sat down, simultaneously exhausted and excited, and she started going on about the whales and all the fish she had seen, all the colors, and how eerie the boat was, and then she said, "When I was a kid we never went on holiday — we couldn't afford it — but this is the most beautiful thing I've ever done. Thank you so much for taking me."

"You're welcome," I said, sitting on my towel, and for a moment she was quiet, staring out at the sea, very satisfied with her adventure. Then she turned and said, with a more serious tone, "Can I tell you something?"

"Sure," I said, with some reluctance, and I felt like a bartender. I could tell that this was one of those moments when a stranger, out of a pressing need, opens up, perhaps inappropriately, to someone they don't know. "What do you want to tell me?"

"I made a terrible mistake coming to Mexico," she said, beginning her confession.

"Why?"

"I've been so dumb."

She stopped and stared out at the water, and I didn't say anything. She had to tell it at her own pace. "So I'm here with a guy," she continued after a deep inhale. "And it's been really bad. I don't really know him, but thank God, we're leaving tomorrow. I just have to get through tonight."

She stopped again, almost seemed on the verge of crying, then said, "Sorry to drop this on you — you don't know me or anything — but I'm all alone, and my phone doesn't really work. The first day it did, but now for three days nothing. I can't even text. I've never been this cut off, and the house doesn't have internet; I can't even email."

"Yeah, there's none of that here *or* much cell phone reception. But one of the rich people, in one of these cliff houses, put up their own cell tower, if you can believe it, and sometimes it works for the rest of us, but most days it doesn't. Seems to depend on the wind."

She nodded, and I realized I wasn't being very comforting, talking about cell phone towers, so I said, "How did you end up down here with someone you don't know that well? Where have you come from? England?"

"No, Los Angeles," she said, and I felt a shiver of anxiety. I had to get back there and sell my house, but I couldn't, I was paralyzed, mired in procrastination, and I zoned out for a second. The girl was still talking. Then I refocused, and she was saying, "I'm from Canterbury, originally, you know, like the poem, Chaucer, but I live in LA now and that's where I met Sebastian."

"Sebastian's the man?"

"Yes."

"So how did you meet him?"

"Because I'm an actress, which means I'm mostly a waitress...Do you actually want to hear this sob story?"

I didn't want to hear it because I didn't like where it was going, but I said, somewhat noncommittally, "If you want to tell me, I can listen."

"Okay...well, it's just pathetic more than anything else. Anyway, he was a customer — I work at this steak house downtown — and he was eating alone, and he told me, after a few glasses of wine, that his girlfriend had broken up with him. A lot of men flirt at that place, even when they're with their wives, but this one, I actually...I don't know, I liked him. Maybe I felt sorry for him. And then at the end of the night — he stayed till closing — he asked me to come to Mexico with him the next day. He had figured out I was an actress and he told me he was a producer. Said he could help me with my career. Biggest cliché ever. And I fell for it."

I was silent, not sure how to respond, and so she kept going. "And he made a big point of saying there was no pressure to sleep together, he just wanted the company and had already rented this place for a trip with his girlfriend and wouldn't be able to get his money back. He showed me pictures of the house and this beach...It looked so beautiful."

She stared out at the water again, and I still didn't know what to say. I managed to eke out, "Has he hurt you?"

She looked at me, a bit shocked. "No, thank God. Nothing like that. Turns out, it wasn't just the two of us coming here. But he failed to mention that part, and so it was a bunch of his friends and their girlfriends, and I think he wanted to show off that he could get somebody at the last minute, a waitress. They all made a big thing of it, that he had picked me up the night before. It was gross — he could have just hired a prostitute — and on top of that they were all doing cocaine the whole time and smoking blues."

"What's that?"

"Smoking blue fentanyl pills, the powder, you sprinkle it on a joint or in a cigarette."

"I didn't know that was a thing."

"Neither did I. I didn't try it. I didn't do any coke, either. I hate cocaine. And they all left this morning, except for us, our flight's tomorrow, and he passed out last night at like seven. Every night, to come down from the coke, he takes a bunch of Valium and sleeps for like twelve hours. Why come all the way here and do that?"

"So, he's not hurt you?"

"No. He's a bit of a cunt," she said dismissively, and I was a little thrown by the word, but then I remembered that the English are fond of it. She continued. "And he's a little mean, but mostly he's been out of it on drugs, and I just thought it would be, I don't know, magical. I've been wanting something special to happen my whole time in LA, you know? And…sorry to dump all this on you, but my mom died at the start of COVID, back in England."

I was taken aback. I managed to say, "I'm very sorry."

"Yeah…She was already pretty sick with emphysema and my dad died a long time ago, so I'm kind of solo in the world now, no family, and I thought maybe somehow this trip was a gift from my mom. Like she wanted me to be happy. I mean, I knew I was taking a risk coming here with him, someone I don't know, but then I thought life is short, I'll just go for it…but…but it's just been so…ugly…they're all just a bunch of trust-fund cokeheads, including him. He's only produced two music videos that nobody's ever seen, and it was with his father's money, anyway, who's some sort of big shot in LA, and one of his friends told me all this behind his back. It was all so gross. They could have been anywhere. They didn't care about the beauty. But *you* saved the whole trip for me. This made it worth it." She smiled at me then and said, "You're a nice person."

I nodded. She didn't know me at all, of course, but maybe my Buddhist studies had made me a good listener, and I felt bad that she was alone in the world. Her pent-up troubles had poured out of her in a rush, but she also seemed resilient. She had that going for her, and I said, "So you just have to get through tonight. What's this man, Sebastian, like, exactly? How old is he?"

"He's older, thirty-six. I'm twenty-eight, and…and he *is* very good-looking, but arrogant. He was so much nicer at the restaurant. He fooled me. But I guess I wanted to be fooled. And I can't believe I'm telling you this, but we've been sleeping in the same bed. But nothing happens, because of the drugs. And I don't want anything to happen. I just want to go home. So crazy to be in one of the most beautiful places in the world and just want to leave."

"Where is he now?"

"He's passed out again. They partied so much. Anyway, that's my sad little story."

I wanted to say something wise and to caution her to be more careful in life, but all I came out with was, "I'm glad you got to snorkel at least."

"So am I," she said, and then I stood up, rather abruptly. All at once, I felt overwhelmed by the conversation and wanted to get back to George and Walter. I wasn't used to this much talking, this much of the troubled world, and I said, somewhat robotically, "Well, I'm going home now. It was nice to meet you, Frances."

She looked surprised that I was ready to go, especially so soon after she had unburdened herself, but then she stood up, and I walked her to the bottom of the white concrete stairs, and she reached out her hand to shake goodbye. She liked to shake hands, it was the tic of a young woman trying to find her way in the world, but then after we shook, she suddenly got up on her toes and kissed me on the cheek and said, "Goodbye, Lou."

Then she turned quickly and, carrying her snorkel bag, she started climbing the stairs.

Feeling a little giddy, I staggered a few feet in the sand, in the direction of home. A woman hadn't kissed me on the cheek in a long time — in fact, I had been celibate for eight years — and then Frances called out to me and said, "Lou, would you like to come sit by the pool and have a drink with me?"

I turned and looked at her.

I had finally been invited up, and I felt like that young man in *The Great Gatsby*, the one who lived next door to all the parties and wondered what it was all about.

I said, "Yes, I'd like a drink very much."

Then I walked back and climbed the stairs to join her.

PART III

1.

I was sitting on one of the lounges, facing the sea, waiting for her to come back with the drinks. I had finally scaled Mount Olympus, and the view from there *was* magnificent. Being elevated did change things, made you feel more prominent yourself somehow, like you were literally on top of the world. And half a mile out, from this heightened rich man's perspective, I saw a pod of gray whales, and a little closer in there was a school of dolphins. I could also see all the way along the cliff line, even south of Dan and Yuko's camp, though I couldn't see the arroyo or their actual camp.

After a few minutes, staring out at the endless sea, I glanced back at the house to see if she was coming with the drinks, but there was no sign of her — the sunlight was blinding off the large plate-glass windows — and when I turned to face the ocean again, I noticed that under the lounge next to me was a movie script of some kind. Curious, I picked it up. The title was *Target Practice for Dying.*

There was a name under the title, which I didn't pay attention to, and I wasn't sure what the title meant, but it seemed pretty good to me. I opened the script to the first page and some of the lines of dialogue were highlighted in yellow, and the name of the character that went with those lines was Monica. Which was an odd coincidence and made me feel strange. Monica was the name of the last woman I had slept with, eight years before, back in 2015, and she was someone I still cared for deeply, though we were no longer in touch. Then I heard Frances say, playfully, "Don't look at that silly script."

I turned and watched her approach, and she handed me my drink and sat on the lounge next to me, where the script had been hiding. I could smell fresh sunblock coming off her skin and, for me, it was the headiest perfume: sunblock smelled like my youth on the beach in San Diego, with all its pretty girls, whom I had loved from afar, and some closer at hand.

Frances reached out her glass to mine — it was pink guava juice with ice and gin — and we clinked. "Cheers," I said.

"You have to look me in the eye," she said, "or... you know."

So I looked her in the eye, and we drank, and I was having sensory overload: the gin, the slight traces of gold-colored hair on her arms, the aphrodisiacal smell of sunblock, and on top of that, the name Monica with all its associations somehow introduced into the mix. I held up the script and said, "Is this a movie you're going to be in? Are you playing Monica?"

She snatched the script from me, acting like she was embarrassed, and said, "Yes, I'm Monica. But I don't know if we'll ever shoot it."

"Why?"

"My friend wrote it and is going to direct it, if he can get the money. He did get one script made, like for half a million. He does low-budget horror, which is kind of big now. But, still, it probably won't happen for years, and then I'll be too old to play the role. But I thought I should bring a script so I could play an actress reading a movie script by a pool, overlooking the Sea of Cortez."

She smiled ruefully at her own fantasy and sipped her drink. Then she said, "This is fun. You're nice to be with." Then she pointed at the whales, threading in and out of the water on the horizon, and said, "I can't believe I got to hear them sing. I didn't even know that was possible."

She offered me her glass for us to clink again in celebration of this, and so we clinked and said cheers. She made sure to look me in the eye, and as I sipped my drink, I heard a man's voice say, very angrily, *"WHO THE FUCK IS THIS?"*

We both swiveled about, swinging our legs around, and coming toward us was a tall, light-haired young man, about my height, with just a white towel wrapped tightly around his midsection. He had a good build on him, like he had rowed crew at one time or was a swimmer. Frances stood up and said, a little nervously, "Sebastian, this is Lou. He took me snorkeling. He lives here."

He stopped in front of us, full of anger, and I stood up from the lounge. I could see why Frances had found him attractive: he was handsome, with rugged masculine features that were on the verge of pretty-boy looks, but what wasn't so nice were the hateful gray eyes, eyes that looked upon the world with an ugly superiority, the kind that usually comes with inherited wealth. I had met plenty of young men with these sorts of eyes, nasty sadists, usually, with deep insecurities because of their powerful fathers, and this one said to Frances, spitting out the words, "What the *fuck* did you do? You picked up some homeless bum?"

"Sebastian," she said, embarrassed. "Please."

Then he turned to me. He had a tall man's arrogance — it wasn't only money that had shaped him, but also his physical gifts — and he appraised me with my wild beard and ragged bathing suit, and said, "What do you do, live in a cave down there?" He gestured with his head to the beach. Then he said, nastily, "Get the fuck out of here."

I felt a left hook wanting to uncoil from my body, not so much for what he had said to me, but for how he had spoken to her, but it's never honorable to coldcock somebody, and so I wondered how I could bait him into taking a swing at *me*. Then my counter would be fair play. But sanity did assert itself, and I said to Frances, "I'm going to take off. Thanks for the drink."

She didn't say anything. I could see she was in pain, and I picked up my satchel with my gear and walked past Sebastian, not crowding him, but not going out of my way. He took a step back, ceding territory, and I looked him in the eye and saw a glimmer of fear.

He was big, but with me right next to him, his brain, on an animal level, made another calculation, not an economic one this time, which had been his first appraisal, and he knew I could hurt him. He glanced away, scared, and I kept going.

At the top of the stairs, I turned, and they were both looking at me, frozen, and I said to her, "Be careful, Frances." She nodded at me, looking quite sad, and then I went down the stairs and out of her life.

Or so I thought.

2.

BACK AT VIC'S HOUSE, I was all out of sorts and looping with worry about the young woman, couldn't put her out of my mind. I wanted to think that Sebastian was mostly harmless, all bark and no bite, and the way he had backed off did indicate that. But they were also all alone now, and my being with Frances had enraged him, and I was terribly worried he'd take his rich-boy anger out on her. She was a much easier target than me, and I kept thinking I should go back there, that I shouldn't have left her with him. *She could stay here,* I thought. I would sleep in the hammock and then drive her to the airport the next day.

She was full of fantasies and had made a young person's bad choice coming down here, which I didn't judge her for: I was fifty-four and still making bad choices, like saying yes to her offer of a drink. If I hadn't gone up there, he wouldn't have seen us and gotten all pissed off. My bad choice had created a ripple, the definition of karma. Now, how could I undo that karma?

The obvious answer was probably to do nothing. To not make things worse.

But my little encounter with the young Englishwoman had stirred things up in all sorts of ways, and finally around eight o'clock, I left Vic's house, having convinced myself that I should check on her. I wanted to make sure she was safe, and if she was all right when I got to the Rock

House — maybe he had passed out again — I would leave her be. But if things seemed bad, then I would offer for her to stay with me, and I'd take her to the airport the next day.

So, in the darkness, not even bringing a flashlight, I headed back to the beach. The desert, as always, was beautifully silent — just the wind and the strange sounds of birds at night, mostly babies crying for their mothers who were out hunting for food.

I was wearing jeans, a T-shirt, and sneakers — the air was still warm — and when I got to the arroyo, Dan and Yuko's fire was dying down. They were in their tent, no light on, already asleep. They lived by the sun, as I had most of my time in Dos Ballenas, and the beach, as I walked to the Rock House, carrying my sneakers, was very dark. With just a meager half-moon in the sky, the world was lit like an X-ray: the white edge of the sea was the line I followed as I trudged north up the sand.

I could have approached the house from the cliff road, but there was a high fence and locked gate off the road, and so I figured I'd just climb back up those Gatsby stairs and see what was going on, see if she was all right.

On some level, I knew this wasn't sane behavior, but I had this feeling that he was going to hurt her, and I needed to stop it.

*   *   *

At the base of the stairs, which glowed whitely in the darkness, I had second thoughts, so I sat on the bottom step, giving myself a chance to reverse course.

I stayed there for several minutes, looking at and listening to the sea, heaving itself against the world. Then comet-like flames began to cross the black sky, before dying in the water.

But I knew they weren't comets: Kathy and Zim would sometimes take mushrooms and send off into the night a dozen or more beautiful Chinese lanterns, made of paper with a candle inside. I had done this with them many times over the last few years, and it was always quite stunning. We would launch a flock of them, one after the other, and in a flaming line, the lanterns would head for the sea, where they would eventually catch fire and burn themselves out.

And that night, sitting on the white steps, I chose to think of the lanterns as an omen, a signal flare from home for me to return.

So I stood up and started walking back, feeling good about my decision not to interfere.

But then I heard something on the wind and convinced myself it was a woman's scream. Then I heard it again and didn't have to convince myself, and I went running up the stairs.

It was Frances who was screaming.

* * *

I crested the top stair, and on the other side of the pool, through the big glass window, I saw her naked, running from him.

During the day, the sun had reflected off the windows, but now I could see that behind the glass was a large living room with long white couches, which Frances was keeping between herself and Sebastian, running from him in a helpless circle.

She shrieked over her shoulder, *"Leave me alone!"*

He wasn't naked like her but was wearing a white robe, and he looked enraged, his face beet red. I sprinted across the deck, which undulated with beams of light from the glowing pool, and on the other side of the window, I saw him catch up to Frances and grab her by the arm. Then he slapped her and she fell to the ground, and he started kicking her. By then I was through the large sliding glass door, which had been left open, and I shouted, *"STOP IT!"*

He whirled, and without hesitation, he charged me, and before I could set myself, he tackled me to the ground, landed on my chest, and started choking me. That was the best thing he could have done, because I reached up and took the index finger of his left hand with my right hand — my strong hand and probably his weak hand — and I snapped his finger, breaking it.

He screamed, and I shoved him off me.

He huddled on the ground, holding his finger, the pain overwhelming him, and I whipped around behind him, like a wrestler, and got him in a chokehold. He struggled like a frenzied animal, but I put him to sleep, being sure not to kill him. Then I turned to Frances. She was still on the floor, on her back, crying and heaving, holding her side where he had kicked her.

I went to her quickly and said, "Let me help you up."

"NO! DON'T TOUCH ME!"

Her mouth was spilling blood — he had split her lip when he hit her — and she curled up into a tight fetal ball to hide her nakedness.

Then she began to rock, like a child, her breath ragged with sobs.

I spied a Mexican blanket on one of the white couches and draped it over her body, and kneeling by her, I tried to comfort her, my hand on her shoulder, but this only made her rock faster. Removing my hand, I said, "I'm so sorry this happened, Frances; when you're ready, let's get you out of here." But she didn't say anything, just kept sobbing, and, in addition to her crying, my head was filled with interior noise, the pounding of fear and adrenaline.

But, then, through all the clamor, I sensed something behind me. I turned and it was Sebastian. He had come to much quicker than I anticipated, and there was a champagne bottle in his good hand, grabbed from a bucket. He started to swing the bottle —

Panicked, I turned away, hoping to avoid the blow, but I was too late.

There was an explosion on the back of my head, followed by the most terrible searing pain, like I had been doused with a bucket of fire.

Then there was no pain, only blackness, then not even that.

3.

LATER, I SAW A pink-red bug high above me, squiggly like a caterpillar, and I started crawling up a long tunnel, at an ascending angle, to get to it. It seemed very important to get to the bug, because if I could get to the bug, I could leave this tunnel, where I was being held captive.

Finally, after much effort, I reached the bug, and my consciousness went to another level of awareness, and I somehow knew that the pink-red bug was actually the edge of my eyelid.

So I sent a message to my brain to lift the eyelid, which it did, good old brain, and I saw a field of white, which didn't make sense at first. Then I became aware of having a body, could place myself in the physical world, and the field of white, I now understood, was one of the couches that Frances had been running around to get away from Sebastian. Then I became even more aware of having a body and realized I was lying *on* the couch, but also lying on something else, and I lifted my head, and it was Frances beneath me.

My face had been in the crook of her neck, flush against the white couch, and, with horror, I pushed off her naked, inert body and fell to the floor. My pants and boxer shorts were at my ankles, and lying on the floor, unable to stand, I thought I might vomit. But I fought that urge, and I reached behind my head. The back of my skull was pulpy and oozing blood, and the pain was grotesque.

Then I looked up, saw one of her feet dangling off the edge of the couch, and I managed to pull up my pants and cover myself. After that, I was able to stand, and I looked down at her, poor broken girl, and knew she was dead. There was a terrible bruise on her neck, indicative that the hyoid bone had been broken.

And I was all too familiar with that specific kind of bruising: it was the mark of death by strangulation. When I was in the LAPD, I had worked out of Hollywood Division, and during my ten-year tour, I had seen at least two hundred dead bodies, primarily ODs and car accident fatalities, but there also had been about a dozen victims of strangulation, mostly prostitutes and a few runaways, and their corpses always had the exact same marking on the neck that Frances now had.

And with my brain slowly getting up to speed, I realized that Sebastian had killed her.

But had set it up to look like I had done it.

He had positioned me between her legs, and he would say he found me on top of her, raping her, strangling her, and that he had snuck up on me — some strange man from the beach who had been coming around that day — and that he had hit me over the head with a champagne bottle to stop me from killing her, but he had been too late.

So if he was staging this, then he was staging it for the police, and I looked at my watch. It was 10:20. I had come to the Rock House around 8:30, which meant I had been out for nearly two hours, and so if Sebastian had managed to contact the police, either in San José del Cabo or La Paz, they would be here very soon.

Adrenalized by anger and fear, I staggered away from her body to find Sebastian, to confront him — and then what, kill him? Was that my only recourse? To kill again? I didn't know, but I had to find the bastard. The house was all lit up, every light on, and I passed through a dining room and into a foyer by the entrance.

There, through a large window by the front door, I could make out a circular drive lit by a spotlight, and in the overflow of that light, I saw him. The big front gate was swung wide open, and he was standing in the middle of the coastal dirt road, waving a flashlight, like a beacon, with the desert behind him an enormous black curtain.

He was now in jeans and a white button-down shirt and was holding a large phone to his ear, a sat phone, which must have come with the house and which he hadn't allowed Frances to use; she said she'd had no contact with anyone for days. As he waved the flashlight, he seemed to be talking to someone on the phone, and I stepped outside.

"Sebastian!" I yelled.

He turned and was visibly frightened to see me. He must have thought he had sent me into a coma, braining me the way he had, and I took a step toward him and shouted, nonsensically, "Why did you kill her?!"

His answer was to drop the flashlight and remove a gun that had been tucked into the back of his pants.

I wasn't expecting that, and he fired at me, hitting the house.

I dashed back through the door, heard another gunshot, and ran back the way I had come and out to the pool. As I approached the staircase down to the beach, I saw on the cliff road, maybe half a mile away, flashing police lights, at least two vehicles. They were south of the arroyo, heading north, and they'd be at the house in less than five minutes.

Then Sebastian, from the living room, fired at me again, exploding the glass window, and I scrambled down the stairs, barely in control, until I hit the beach and fell to the sand. But I got to my feet and started running in the darkness, heading for Dan and Yuko's camp and the arroyo, a quarter mile away, but then fell again.

I looked back. Sebastian didn't seem to be following me, but soon the cops would be in pursuit, and I got to my feet and ran, but then I collapsed again, and this time I couldn't get up. For at least a minute, I lay there, unable to move, my head pounding.

Then I heard men shouting to each other, and at the top of the stairs, I saw the beams of flashlights: the police! That got me up and moving, and I was sure they couldn't see me in the darkness: I was already too far away. But they'd catch me before long—I was hardly able to move in the sand — and not knowing what else to do, I slipped into the water as quietly as I could.

This was my worst nightmare, swimming in the ocean at night, but I shed my pants and shirt, so as to not be waterlogged. The cold water was an extreme jolt to my nervous system, but it also brought me to life, and I started swimming out: I kept my head low and did a breaststroke. Then as the water got deeper, I looked back, and I could see the silhouettes of two men descending the stairs, their flashlights leading the way. There was still no chance they could see me — my hair was dark and my skin was dark — but I stayed low in the water and swam farther out, unknown beasts lurking beneath me.

When I had made it about fifty yards, about halfway to the rocks that jutted out of the sea, I looked back again, and the two men were at the bottom of the stairs, flashlights probing the beach, looking for me. Then the beams of light swung out to the water, but I was much too far out to be seen — their lights couldn't reach that far.

Nevertheless, I stayed very still, treading water, and then the two policemen, unsure which direction I had run, started jogging up the sand to the north, their flashlights giving them away. This was a bit of luck on a very unlucky night, and I watched them for about a minute. Then, with the wind and surf covering any sounds I might make, I began to swim toward the south, parallel to the shore, heading for Dan and Yuko's camp.

And as I swam, leaving a skein of blood in my wake, I could feel the sharks beneath me.

So I had no sense of time.

Only terror.

4.

IN AN ALTERED STATE, infused with adrenaline, I ran along the dirt roads back to Vic's house. I had survived the nightmarish swim, and barefoot, wearing only my boxer shorts, I had to cover only about a mile, my daily jog. I kept expecting to see flashing police lights, but they must have been still searching for me on the beach. They might have even found my pants and shirt washed up and wondered if I had drowned.

But soon, no matter what, they'd fan out, rouse someone, and ask where the American with the beard lived. That would be how Sebastian would describe me: a fiftysomething American with an unruly black-and-silver beard, and most of the expats would know my description, as well as the name I had given them: Lou Brink. To them, I was Vic's friend, the guy who had been COVID-squatting in his place for three years.

So I didn't have much time — it had been at least thirty minutes since the cops had shown up — and as I jogged down Vic's dirt driveway, I approached the house cautiously, because maybe they had already found me.

But there were no police vehicles in front of the house, just Vic's red Toyota, which was going to be my ticket out of Dos Ballenas. My plan was to get George and Walter, put on some clothes, grab the car keys, and flee. A simple plan. My only plan.

Thinking it safe, I rushed to the house, opened the front door, and turned on the lights.

And waiting for me, standing by the kitchen table, were two men in jeans and thin leather jackets. They had guns pointed in my direction, and I thought, almost nonchalantly, *Oh, shit, the cops are here.*

One man was skinny and ugly, and one was round and ugly, and the skinny one waved his gun at me, a .38, and said, "Get on your knees, asshole."

And I realized these weren't Mexican cops. They were something else bad.

They took a few steps closer to me, and George, not reading the room, raced over and jumped on me, and the skinny one, who had a long waxy nose, thrust the .38 at my head and said, "Forget the fucking dog, get on your fucking knees."

So I got on my knees, and George, happy to have me on his level, started licking the blood that was still leaking from the back of my head and down my neck, and I said, "Okay, George…enough, George," and I gently pushed him away, and George, not perceiving that these men were enemies, trotted back over to the bed and lay down with Walter.

"Cute dog," said the other man, who looked like an old-timey wrestler, swarthy, fat, and mean. Then he gestured at me with his gun, a .22, and said, "What the fuck happened to you?"

He was referring to the fact that I was practically naked and had a gaping wound on the back of my head. I said, "I went for a late-night swim and a shark bit me."

He didn't like that and so he came up to me and hit me across the face with the barrel of his pistol. I gave a little cry of pain — how could I not? — and I reached up to my cheek and blood came through my fingers.

"Easy, easy," said the skinny one to his partner, and he seemed to be the alpha. An ugly-as-hell alpha. He had receding red hair and a sucked-in, chinless face, to go with his thin, waxy nose, which was the kind with a lot of pinholes in it. He also had a pink scar on his left cheek that looked like a worm half dead on a sidewalk after a rain. But that wormy scar also looked a hell of a lot like the scar I used to have before the doctor removed it, and this gave me a weird feeling.

"Don't tell me what to do," said the wrestler, who might have been shaving since birth — the back of his neck had a thick pelt of black hair.

Wax-nose made a calming motion with his .38 and said, "Just simmer down. I'm going to call Kunian, get an ID, and *then* you can pop him and work out your anger. Okay?"

Kunian. The sex trafficker. The sixty thousand bucks I had stolen back in 2020. That's what this was. So all my karma was coming due tonight. New karma. Old karma. Bad karma.

But I didn't have time for this right now. The Mexican cops would be here soon.

Except I couldn't make a move: the dark-haired wrestler, keeping his temper under control, had the .22 pointed at my head, while wax-nose took out his phone and hit a button and held the thing in front of his face, followed by that FaceTime ringing sound. Then the ringing stopped, and from the phone I heard a gruff voice say, "What's happening?"

"We found him. Middle of fucking nowhere in Baja. And he's all fucked up, I don't know why. He was out swimming in the ocean or something. So make the ID and we'll...you know."

I guess he was keeping it clean for anybody who might be listening or watching, unlikely as that was, and then wax-nose put his phone in front of me, and on the screen, I saw a shriveled old man in a white T-shirt at a desk. It seemed like someone else was holding the phone in front of him, and this old man was looking at me and studying me.

Then he lifted his arms in frustration, and I saw that he had no hands — his arms were stumps — and he said, "I can't fucking tell if it's him!"

Wax-nose turned the phone back around and said to the old man, "I told you that doc gave him a new face, but how good a job could it be?"

And another tumbler dropped. *The doctor.* Somehow, he got them on to me.

"So look again," said wax-nose to the phone, and he put the thing back in front of me. I realized then that the shriveled old man was Jack Kunian himself, but I hadn't recognized him. When I had met him three years before, he had probably weighed close to four hundred pounds, but since then he had lost two-thirds of his mass. *And his hands.*

Kunian said, "Are you the fucking bastard who did this to me?"

He raised his arms and I didn't say anything.

So the wrestler shoved the barrel of his .22 into the wound in the back of my head, and I screamed. He removed the gun and said, "Fucking talk to the man."

"I don't know what's going on," I said, playing scared, though it wasn't that much of an act. "I don't know who you guys think I am —"

Then they lost the signal. It was a miracle it had lasted that long.

"Fuck," said wax-nose, and he hit the button again, and Kunian came back. The wind was in their favor: the privately owned cell tower was working. For the time being.

"What happened?" Kunian said.

"Fucking cell phones, that's what happened," said wax-nose. "So you good? We do our thing and come collect?" He was eager to move on. Make his money.

"No!" said Kunian. "I'm not sure it's him. Bring him to me. I need to look him in the eye. Then I'll know."

"No fucking way."

"I'll pay."

"Forget about it. We do it now and you pay us when we see you."

"But I need to know for sure! What good is it if I'm not sure? I've been waiting for this for years. How much more will it cost me?"

Wax-nose glanced at his partner, and the wrestler whispered, "Let's just pop him. We got the other buyer."

I didn't know what the hell that meant, another *buyer,* but I was going to have to make a move soon. Wax-nose said to Kunian, "Listen, I'm gonna be frank with you. We have a second client for this piece of shit. So, to make it worth my while, to drag this bum all the way across the border, it's an additional fifty K."

"You're double-dipping?" said Kunian.

"That's right. No law against it. You still get what you paid for. And somebody else gets what they paid for."

"Who's the somebody else?"

"That's not relevant."

There was silence. Then Kunian said, "Twenty-five more."

"Fifty," said wax-nose. "Twenty-five of that alone will go for the service in TJ. No way I can take him across the border legally; too complicated."

There was silence again, then Kunian said, "Okay. An additional fifty large. Seventy-five total. And find out this bastard's name. We can track down any family he has and there'll be more work for you, you greedy —"

Then the connection died again.

"Fuck, fuck," said wax-nose, and he tried calling back. But it didn't go through; he tried several times, but nothing. I didn't tell him that it might not work again for days, and I said, stalling, "What is this about? You got the wrong guy. I don't know what's going on —"

"Shut up," said the wrestler, and made like he was going to hit me again, but didn't, though it made him laugh to see me flinch.

Then wax-nose, frustrated, put his phone away, giving up on it. He took plastic cuffs out of his pocket, handed them to the wrestler.

"Cuff him, then let's get out of here," he said, and he went off to the side so he could shoot me without winging his partner if I made a move.

They were half decent pros, not great, and from my kneeling position, I slumped submissively and put my hands out in front of me. And maybe because I looked half dead already, the wrestler then made a big mistake and did as I had hoped: cuffed me in front.

Wax-nose said, "What's your name, asshole? Boss man wants to know. We can beat it out of you, or you can just tell us."

"My name's Lou Brink and my passport's under the mattress," I said, wanting to seem compliant. "I'll get it. And you'll see you got the wrong guy."

I stood up, hands cuffed in front, but wax-nose wasn't having it and said, "Don't fucking move." Then he said to the wrestler, "Check under the mattress."

So the wrestler went over to the bed, with George and Walter eyeing him, and he put his gun in the back of his pants and knelt down. Then he lifted the mattress, dug his hand underneath, and came out with the sharpened, gleaming machete I had hidden there for a moment like this.

"Holy shit," he said, admiring it, and the shiny machete distracted wax-nose as well, so I spun around and chopped at his .38 with my bound hands and knocked it to the ground.

Then I drove him in the direction of the wall, like we were dance partners, and George finally got into the act, realizing these men weren't pals. He threw all twenty-four of his pounds against wax-nose, snarling and biting, and when I had wax-nose against the wall, I viciously head-butted him, and he crumpled to the floor.

When I turned, the wrestler was charging me with the machete, forgetting the gun in the back of his pants, and I dove at his knees, upending him like a bowling pin, and he flipped in the air. The machete went flying, and he landed on his back, gasping for breath, the wind knocked out of him, and I came out of my dive, spun around, and delivered three concussive hammerblows with my cuffed fists to the center of his face until he was unconscious.

Meanwhile, wax-nose, all fucked up, was crawling for his gun. I stomped on his head with the heel of my right foot, and he went to sleep. I then collected their guns — found two more on their ankles — and put all the weapons on the kitchen table. After that, I fired up the little burner on the stove, held the plastic cuffs to the flame, and snapped them off, easy.

And all the while, there had been noise in my head, like a high-pitched scream, but then it quieted down, and I looked around me: the two men were unconscious but looked to be breathing. At least I hadn't killed again, and George had gotten back onto the bed with Walter, and they were both licking themselves as a way to deal with their nerves after all the excitement.

Then I opened the front door to see if the Mexican cops were coming, but there was still no sign of them, no flashing lights, and I realized that there was something maybe good in all this, these two guys showing up. *If I moved quickly.*

5.

I RAPIDLY BOUND THEIR hands with two sets of plastic cuffs I had found in wax-nose's jacket pockets, where I also found what I had actually been looking for: car keys. While I cuffed wax-nose, I noticed a protrusion under his shirt: a loaded money belt. Which I relieved him of.

Then I went outside. Their car, a ten-year-old black Lincoln, was hidden behind the house. I pulled it around to the front, popped the trunk, and nearly had a heart attack. The mechanic from La Paz — the one I had sold my Chevy to, Felix Rosales — was in the trunk and very dead. He was still wearing his thick black glasses, but now there was a third eye in the middle of his forehead that would never need glasses.

And I might as well have pulled the trigger myself.

Because of me, he had been executed. And what of Frances? If I hadn't gone up for that drink...if I hadn't gone back to the house...Would *she* be alive? Typhoid Doll...come near me and...

But I couldn't think about these things right now — my karma, my complicity — and so I shoved the mechanic to the back of the trunk, deep into the well. It was a good-size trunk, because then I managed to get wax-nose and the wrestler in there with the dead man, bending their limbs a little cruelly, and both men woke up during the transfer and were screaming as I slammed the trunk closed.

After that, I got dressed real fast — khaki pants, T-shirt, sandals, and my sweater — and put George and Walter in the front seat of the car, along with the four guns, my burner phone, and wax-nose's money belt.

Then I dug up the lockbox by the palapa, which held my wallet, my passport, and my dead cell phone, the only links that Happy Doll had to this place. There was also about eight hundred dollars cash in the box — all there was to my name — but I left the money in the lockbox, went back in the house, and planted it under the bed. One more reason for the cops to think I was still around — either drowned or hiding somewhere — and with a loaded money belt I didn't need that cash anymore.

I went to the door to leave and looked back at the big room that had been our home, and I had the presence of mind to say goodbye, to thank it for three good years…up till now. Then I remembered there was some Krazy Glue in the kitchen, and I grabbed it to put on the back of my head later, *and* I snatched up a bottle of Don Julio.

Finally, tequila in hand, I got the hell out of there and closed the door, leaving as I had arrived: *In trouble. On the run.*

This all had taken about ten minutes — ten minutes I didn't really have — and I started the Lincoln, then had another thought, which was going to slow me down some more but seemed important. So I got out of the car and with the butt of wax-nose's .38, I smashed the red brake lights and scattered the shards in the dirt.

After that, I drove the Lincoln out of there with no headlights on, and at the end of Vic's long driveway, I turned right on the east-west road, heading west for the mountains. The cops would be coming from the east, from the cliff house, and with the brake lights smashed I would be practically invisible as I crossed the dark plain.

But it was so dark, I could barely make out the narrow road, and I was worried about driving off the hardpack and getting stuck in the softer desert sand, which meant I couldn't go too fast, less than thirty miles an hour. And a minute into the journey, a quarter mile from Vic's, I saw in the rearview mirror the flashing lights of the two police vehicles.

They had finally been told where the large, bearded American lived, and

I stopped the car. I thought it was too dark for them to see me, but there was even less chance of a car's shape being spotted on the horizon if it was still and not kicking up dirt. Then the police cars turned off the road and went down Vic's driveway, before coming to a stop in front of his house, which I could see in the spill of their headlights.

But I couldn't see if men were getting out of the cars — it was too far an expanse. Then the lights of the two cars were killed…

And I waited a minute…then another thirty seconds…They must have gone into the house, and so I continued driving west, no lights on, no brake lights, a phantom.

When I got to the base of the mountains, I put my lights on and turned north. There were no roadblocks along the way, and no one seemed to be in pursuit. I had left behind the red Toyota, money, and the clothing on the beach. They thought I was either dead or gone to ground; there would be no way they could know that two assassins had shown up and provided me with a getaway vehicle, a Lincoln with a deep trunk.

So, fueled by adrenaline, I drove well into the night, with George and Walter on the front seat next to me, boon companions, unflappable and loving.

On the back seat were two smallish travel bags — I'd go through those later — and a carton of water bottles, which was good: I didn't want George and Walter to get dehydrated.

I wasn't sure exactly where I was headed, except to get as far away as possible in a northerly direction, and for a while, as we careened through the desert on bumpy dirt roads, the two men in the trunk could be heard intermittently screaming.

But then, as time went on, there were no more screams.

Though I hoped they weren't dead because I had a lot of questions.

6.

Around 5:30 a.m., predawn, with the sky turning pink, we drove through the small coastal city of Loreto, which had paved roads and stores but at that time of day was still very much asleep. Which was what I needed: sleep. I was on the verge of collapse, and on the northern outskirts of the town, I found a boarded-up old church and parked in the back. The two buildings alongside the church, a market and a gas station, were also abandoned, and so there was a lot of privacy: no one would know we were there.

I was pretty sure I had a concussion — a few hours before I had poured tequila on the wound and had Krazy Glued it closed — and I wondered if I might die if I slept, but there was no getting around it: I had to rest. But first I let George and Walter out so they could do their business, and while they sniffed about the dirt lot, I opened the money belt and did a quick count: I was now twenty-five grand richer, which was going to help me get back to the States.

But that was a long way off yet. It was at least six hundred miles to the border.

So I got the animals back in the car, reclined the driver's seat, and slept for about four hours. I woke up with the sun baking me through the front window, and I thought, *I guess I'm still alive.*

Which isn't your usual first thought of the day, and as I came to, my head was killing me. I thought to check the bags on the back seat for pain pills or aspirin, but first I wanted to see if the bags' owners were still alive. That seemed to be a more important order of business, and I grabbed the .22, just in case one of them sprang out at me. When I popped the trunk, I was hit by a gush of bad smells: feces, urine, and corpse.

But only one corpse.

Wax-nose and the wrestler were passed out but not dead: they were breathing, raggedly.

And all three men were on their sides, knees bent, lined up like fish in a tin: the dead mechanic was spooning the wrestler, and the wrestler was spooning wax-nose.

I dug around in the hit men's jackets and removed their wallets, which I should have done earlier. They both had California driver's licenses with Riverside addresses. Wax-nose was Lucas Poole, age forty-eight, and the dark-haired wrestler was Marco Venturi, age forty-two.

They also had what looked like official bounty hunter licenses, which meant they played on both sides of the tracks, and between the two wallets was a thousand American dollars and the equivalent in pesos. I also took their phones, but both were dead, having lost their charge, and I wondered what, ultimately, I should do with these two men. A main tenet of Buddhism is to love and revere others. Compassion, even for the most horrid and flawed, is the goal.

In essence, you're to love your neighbor *more* than yourself.

But could I love and revere these two? These killers? Maybe if I imagined them as children. Which I did for a moment. I saw them as small boys, running in a yard, sweet and innocent. They hadn't always been bad, but then the vision faded, and I reached in and tapped them pretty hard on their cheekbones with the butt of the .22.

That woke them up, but they were weak and half delirious, not quite with it. On top of being jostled for hours on dirt roads, they had been baking in the trunk since the sun came up. *And* I had smashed in their faces the night before.

So I fed them some water, and with their hands cuffed behind their backs, they strained up to the bottle, like little birds in a nest. I felt almost tender and maternal bottle-feeding them this way, and the hydration unscrambled their brains a little. The wrestler, Venturi, in a hoarse whisper, said, "I'm gonna kill you, you motherfucker."

But Poole, he of the wax nose and the livid facial scar, didn't say anything, just looked at me with hatred, and I gave him some more water.

Then he whispered, "Where are you taking us? Why are you doing this?"

"Why did you kill the mechanic?"

"I didn't. He did."

"Fuck you, Lucas."

"Why did *you* kill him, then?" I said, looking at Venturi, but it was Poole who answered.

"Because he didn't want to pay him what we agreed to for acting as our guide. Thought it was easier to kill him. I was against it."

"You bastard," said Venturi bitterly, and lying behind Poole, he tried to head-butt him, but it was ineffective: he was too weak. They were turning on each other, and Poole said, "Let me out of here. We can work something out."

"Sure," I said, and I slammed the trunk shut and went into the back seat to look through their bags. Unfortunately, there were no pain pills; between the two bags there was just a bunch of weird, useless private crap: fungus creams, Cialis, medicated ass wipes, chewable Pepto.

But Venturi's bag, which I could tell was his by the waist size of the underwear, did yield something I could use. At the bottom, under an iPad, which he probably had just for pornography, was a ziplock bag with weed, a pipe, and a lighter. Just what the doctor ordered.

I smoked several bowls and sipped a little tequila, and the combo lessened my headache considerably. I was eager to start driving again, but I figured I should get some answers first. Holding on to the .22, I popped the trunk and said, "How did you find me? I want details."

Venturi said, "Fuck you, I'm gonna kill you someday." I nodded and went to the back seat and got one of his own stinky T-shirts out of his bag. I came back around to the trunk and shoved the T-shirt deep in his mouth. He choked for a minute, then got the hang of breathing through his nose.

But then his eyes rolled back in his head, and I pulled the T-shirt out. He wasn't dead, but he had passed out. He'd had a rough night.

I pointed the gun at Poole and said, "*You* gonna talk?"

"Will you let me go? I know you took my money belt, but you can keep it. All of it."

"You tell me everything and I'll cut you loose right here. You still don't know my name. You'll never find me again."

"That's right," he said, desperate. "That's right. I'll never find you."

"We have a deal, then: you talk and you live."

He nodded. Wanted to believe me. He had what's called "the illusion of reprieve," which I had read about in a book on the Holocaust. The writer of the book, an Auschwitz survivor, said that most of his fellow prisoners had this deluded hope that they would be saved, and, oddly, it was the ones who *didn't* have this hope, who didn't have the "illusion of reprieve," who were the most likely to survive.

But maybe Poole wasn't deluded. Maybe I wasn't going to kill him—I didn't want to do that anymore—and I told him to start from the beginning.

So, fighting for his life, he gave me the whole story.

He said that he and Venturi were legit bounty hunters, but that was mostly cover and they made their real bank tracking down bad guys for bad guys, with contract killing sometimes part of the equation. And on behalf of the Sinaloa Cartel, they had been in Tijuana and Rosarito looking for a coke mule, a stripper with an American passport who had gone missing with a million bucks' worth of high-grade cocaine.

The coke, in glycine bags, had been hidden in the stripper's breast implants and her buttocks implants—that's how she transported the product once or twice a year—and Poole and Venturi had been going around to all the chop-shop medicos, on both sides of the border, looking for someone who might have opened her up. The Sinaloas figured the stripper was trying to rip them off and peddle the coke on her own, or she had been kidnapped by bad actors with the same intention. Either way, a doctor would be needed, and not a straight doctor.

Which brought Poole and Venturi to Casa Feldman. The doc said he had nothing to do with the stripper, and after they beat him up pretty good, they figured he was telling the truth. And that would have been the end of it, but the doc, looking to make a buck after his beating, to make it worth his while, offered to remove Poole's facial scar, at a discounted price.

Poole said, "It was crazy. We kick the shit out of him, and he wants to work on my face, and I told him to forget about it. But he didn't listen, said he could remove the scar like it had never been there, that it would improve my looks, and then he said he had removed a scar just like mine one time, had done a beautiful job on a guy. And that rang a bell in my head —"

Poole started coughing then, and when he was finished, he rasped, "Give me some more water." I nursed him with the bottle, and when he had his fill, he closed his eyes, like he was going to pass out. So I leaned into the trunk, put the .22 against his forehead, and said, "Keep talking."

He opened his eyes, and I pulled the gun back. "Okay, okay," he said. "I'm telling you everything. We have a deal, right?"

"Yeah. So when was it you saw the doctor and he told you about the scar?" Venturi was snoring now, loudly, but we both ignored it.

"That was like three days ago, and it rang a bell because back in January 2020, Kunian hired us to find...you. And he said you had a scar just like mine. But we never could track you down — COVID hit, the whole world went to shit — and Kunian gave up. But he had wanted you bad. You ripped him off, right?"

"That's right."

"Except it wasn't his money. You know that? It was a big dose of Jalisco cash. Sixty K or something. And they chopped off one of his hands as a lesson. But because of the sixty K, they realized he'd been skimming for a while, and they took off his other hand."

"But they didn't kill him."

"Alive, he sends a better message to the others...Anyway, I asked the Russian doctor when he had done this work, removing a scar like mine, and he realized he had said too much...and —"

Poole clammed up then, and I said, "And what? You beat him up some more? I'm fond of that doctor."

"Yeah, well, we had to make him talk, like you're making me talk, and he said you'd been there three years before, that he'd given you a whole new face, which clocked when Kunian would have been looking for you and why you'd want a new...*look,* and so then I asked that Russian doctor where you were, but he said he had no idea..."

So Poole and Venturi beat him up some more, and the doc told them that he had dropped me *and* a little dog off at a parking garage down in Rosarito but swore that was the last time he had ever seen me. By then he was in bad shape, and Poole and Venturi didn't think he was holding out, and so they went down to the garage in Rosarito to prowl around, to see if they could pick up my scent.

And lucky for them, the same attendant still worked there, and he actually did remember a tall American with a dog, and what helped him remember was that my car, a beautiful '85 Chevy, had a dead battery. Then Poole got a hold of the mechanic who had jump-started the car, and that guy also remembered the car and the dog *and* that he had given me directions to La Paz.

After that, they called Kunian back in the States to find out if he was interested in renewing his contract on me — since they had a pretty good lead — and Kunian was all for it. He agreed to pay twenty-five K for proof of death, up five K in three years, *inflation,* and their next move was to head down to La Paz, where they planned to go around to every auto shop in town, about a dozen places.

Their reasoning was that an '85 Chevy might have had more problems, and they got lucky again. The fifth auto shop they went to was the one where Vic had taken his Toyota and where I met the mechanic, Felix Rosales, who later bought my Chevy, and of course Felix remembered me when Poole asked him. Nine months before, in the spring of 2022, I had driven the Caprice to La Paz, and after the sale, for a hundred bucks, cutting into my profit, Felix had driven me back to Dos Ballenas, and during the ride, he had told me about his wife and two little daughters.

"So that's how we found you," said Poole. "The mechanic remembered how to get to your place. More or less. Ninety minutes down the coast on dirt roads and then you make a right at some point, near the big rocks on the plain, like whales. Then you look for a yurt and after the yurt would be your dump, and so once we found the yurt, we found you."

"I left breadcrumbs."

"Yeah…and we had some luck. Now I've told you everything. So let me out of here. Like I said, you can keep the money belt."

"That's generous of you," I said, and I leaned into the trunk and pointed the .22 at his forehead. "But you left out part of the story. Who's the other client that wants me dead?"

Poole looked away then, scared, caught in a lie.

So I shoved the .22 in his mouth, a gross act, but effective, and when I took it out, he told me that the doc hadn't just told them about the parking garage: he also told them about Diablo. That I had killed him. Which prompted Poole to call his contact with the Sinaloas, who sent things up the chain of command, and what came back was an offer of twenty-five K for my head, the going rate, and since there were multiple teams looking for the coke mule, he and Venturi were free to go to La Paz and hunt for me.

I said, "What did you do to the doc to get him to talk about Diablo?"

Poole hesitated, and I pointed the .22 back at his head, and he said, "Marco killed his son. He was retarded or something and fought back. That's when the doctor told us everything."

For a moment, I was stunned. They had killed Ivan.

Then I slammed the trunk closed and started driving.

Poole screamed for a little while but then stopped.

I wanted to go see the doc, and it was a pathetic gesture, but I thought I'd give him the money belt. It was the least I could do. But I could also give him the two men. His son's killers. If he wanted to, we could drive them off of Diablo's cliff.

Which meant there would be no more illusion of reprieve.

For any of us.

7.

I DIDN'T CALL AHEAD on my burner phone because maybe the doc wouldn't want to see me; I had brought him enough misery.

So my plan was to just show up, though I stopped a few times on the way there for gas and food and to keep the two men alive. I gave them water and hand-fed them beef gorditas, which I had picked up at a roadside stand, and they accepted the nourishment: all the fight had gone out of both of them. It was hard work being tied up in a trunk, hours on end, maybe even fatal, but it was important to me that they not die. I wanted the doctor to determine their fate, and we pulled into Casa Feldman around ten o'clock at night.

By that point, I was practically hallucinating with fatigue — it had been a hideous twenty-four hours, even by the violent standards of my life — and I parked in front of the main house of the old hunting lodge. There were no lights on, and no lights on in any of the cabins, but the doctor's pickup truck was there, and I figured that he and his wife and the nurses were all asleep.

I didn't like waking them, but I wasn't going to wait till morning, and with the headlights of the Lincoln lighting the way, I went to the front door and knocked loudly. I waited but there was no response, and I knocked again. Then I noticed that the dogs, who lived outside in a shed, with old blankets on the floor, didn't come running. Something was off, so I tried the knob of the front door — it wasn't locked — and let myself in.

The lights from the car, coming through the open door, partially illuminated the front area of the house, which was half sitting room, half dining room.

There was a smell in the air, and I called out, "Doctor, are you home?"

But there was no response — the place felt empty of life. I reached for a light switch on the wall, flipped it up, and off to the left, there they were, all lined up on the floor, like dead soldiers after a battle: the doctor, his wife, his son, and the two elderly nurses.

And they each had a bullet hole in the center of the forehead.

They had been shot the same way as Felix, the mechanic, with a .22, point-blank. I could tell because the holes were relatively small, and that's what .22s are for: execution work, up close, and that was the kind of gun Venturi carried.

I walked over to the bodies to get a closer look, and the doctor's eyes were still open, but all the things he had seen were now lost to the world.

How naive I had been. The twenty-five thousand dollars in the money belt. Why else would Poole be carrying that much cash in Mexico? Before coming to Dos Ballenas, he and Venturi must have been paid by the Sinaloa for offing the doctor and his family, delayed retribution for Diablo, and then when they bagged me, they'd collect another twenty-five K.

But Kunian's offer of seventy-five K to drag me back to the States, before whacking me, had been too good to pass up. And so they had hoped to make seventy-five off Kunian, plus twenty-five from the Sinaloa... double-dipping.

No law against it, Poole had said on the phone to Kunian.

I left the bodies and went back to the car and reclined the seat, needing to think, to collect myself. George and Walter crawled all over me, loving me, which gave me strength.

Then I got out of the car and popped the trunk, which had an interior light.

Felix was still very dead, and my two hostages were unconscious. I got a bottle of water and threw it on them, and they sputtered awake.

I said, half sane, "Is there anyone who loves you?"

I had the half cocked idea that if they were loved that maybe I should somehow spare them, but they looked at me blankly. Then Venturi said, "Please, mister, let us out. I can't feel my arms. I can't feel anything. *Please.*"

It was eerily regressed, him calling me mister. He was completely Stockholmed and broken, and I said, "Don't worry, I'm thinking about what to do with you."

Poole whispered, hoarsely, "Where are we?"

"Near Tijuana," I said, and they, of course, had no idea where I had taken them: the dark forest around us was quiet and a bit chilly, and the only lights in the woods were the Lincoln's headlights shining on the house and the little trunk light shining on the three men: two dying, one dead.

"Let us go," said Poole. "We'll never look for you. I promise."

Of course he was lying. They would look for me day and night, but I said, "Okay. I won't kill you. I promise. You just have to give me some more information."

"What more can I tell you?"

Well, there were a few things that came to mind, and in the glove compartment, I found a pen and an old handbook for the Lincoln. I took that back out to the trunk and opened the book so I could write everything down on the blank inside cover. Then I asked Poole and Venturi for the following items: the passcodes to their phones and the passwords to their bank accounts, linked to the ATM cards in their wallets.

They obediently gave me everything, and then I asked them where Kunian lived, and they didn't know, but they knew where he worked. He owned a strip club in Riverside, called Diamond Dancers, and they said he was there all the time. The place was a laundry for the Jalisco Cartel, and Poole said Kunian still worked for the Jaliscos, cleaning their money and distributing product, even after what they had done to him: cutting off his hands for stealing.

"Nice people to work for," I said, and the final thing I wanted from these two was information about the service in Tijuana that Poole had mentioned on the phone to Kunian, the service that could get people across the border: I needed to know how it worked.

Clinging to hope, they didn't hold anything back, and I wrote it all down. When they finished spilling, I closed the book and said, "This has been very helpful. Now, what's going to happen is, I'm not going to kill you, like I promised. I'm trying not to do that anymore, but I *am* going to close this trunk and leave you here and maybe you can figure a way out. I know this seems cruel…and it is…But think about all the things you have done that have led to this moment. That's your karma coming to fruition, and if you somehow survive, which would also be your karma, never do those things again. Because if you do, you will have even worse karma. I know that's hard to imagine. But it's how things work."

I reached up then to close the trunk, and this wasn't at all a Buddhist solution, but I was more endarkened than enlightened, more nuts than sane, and Poole, his face falling apart, looking like the little boy I had envisioned earlier in the day, said, "Please don't do this. *Please.*"

It was unsettling, his face shattering like that, revealing the child buried within, and it gave me pause. Then I looked at Venturi, who simply closed his eyes and couldn't even summon the energy to beg: he was done.

"Please," said Poole, again. *"Please."*

"You shouldn't have killed the mechanic," I said. "You shouldn't have killed the doctor and his family."

Poole's eyes widened — I had caught him in another lie — and he saw the silhouettes of the trees behind me and understood now where I had taken them: to the doctor's lodge in the middle of nowhere. "They were old," he pleaded. "We did them a favor, and the son…that was no way to live."

I nodded politely and said, "I have to go now," and finding my resolve, I slammed the trunk closed. Poole shrieked once but then stopped, probably too weak to cry out more than that, and on unsteady legs, I went into the house, where I found the doctor's keys to his truck.

After that, I transferred George and Walter into the pickup and drove us out of the dark forest, one step closer to home.

8.

In Tijuana, a little after midnight, I checked into the Motel Coronado, which was a few blocks in from the beach and not far from the city's famous bullring, Plaza Monumental de Playas de Tijuana, known in English, famously, as the Bullring by the Sea.

Fortunately, the Coronado, a nice little place, accepted animals, and it was on a busy street of restaurants and bars, all open late.

Our small, tidy room was on the second floor, and when we got to the room, George right away jumped on the bed, like a child, eager to play, but Walter, less excitable and more world-weary, simply went into the bathroom and drank from the toilet. In his all-white suit, he made everything look elegant.

Exhausted, I quickly got undressed, and when I turned off the bedside lamp, the headlights of cars leaked through the metal blinds on the window and played on the ceiling, like roving spotlights in a prison yard. But it didn't matter. I soon passed out and slept for almost twelve hours, with George against my torso and Walter on top of my head.

When I woke up, midday, I felt all right, considering everything, but a little while later, at a walk-in clinic, I had the back of my skull looked at, just in case, and they shaved off a bunch of hair and cleaned away the excess Krazy Glue, which had done a good job closing the wound, without infection. There was still a big, hideous lump I could feel with my fingers, but I didn't have a fractured skull or any kind of brain leak, which I took as good news, and in my limited Spanish, I told the physician I had been in a bar brawl. This was par for the course for an American in Tijuana, and he shook his head, barely paying attention.

After the clinic, I went to a barber shop and got the rest of my hair buzzed down to a salt-and-pepper nub, and they also removed my beard. I thought it was unlikely, but if the cops were looking for an American of my description, it wasn't a bad idea to change my look.

The next thing on the agenda was the internet. At a hotel on the beach, the Del Mar, I snuck into the business office, but I couldn't find anything on the web about a young Englishwoman named Frances being murdered in Dos Ballenas. Not having her last name didn't help things internet-wise, but back in LA, I'd do a more exhaustive search to find out who Frances was, as well as find out if the Mexican police were looking for "Lou Brink" or if he was presumed dead.

From the Del Mar, I ran two more errands: at a tourist shop, I bought a black baseball cap that said *Tijuana* across the front, in purple script. I wanted the hat to cover my new scar, because anyone standing behind me was in for a nasty shock. Then at the Mexican equivalent of a dollar store, I bought a mesh beach purse with a zipper, to act as a cat carrier for Walter. It only came in one color, bright pink.

And doing all this, being out in the world, was nerve-wracking: the hordes of gaseous motorbikes alone had me jumping out of my skin. After three years of near isolation, I felt like a Buddhist Rip Van Winkle woken from my slumber.

I mean, I had been on brief supply runs to La Paz and San José del Cabo during my time in Mexico, but they were small towns compared to Tijuana, which is home to more than two million people and probably four million motorbikes.

To calm myself down, I was going to stop in a bar for a tequila, but it started pouring, and I decided to run back to the motel. Evening was coming on fast — the days were January short — and, back in the room, I stripped out of my wet clothes and sipped a little of my own tequila to warm up. Then, still on task, ticking off my mental to-do list, I texted Kunian from Poole's phone, stating that we'd had car trouble and wouldn't be back in Riverside for four or five days, depending on how long it took to get the car fixed.

I did this to buy myself some time, because I didn't know what I was going to do about Kunian, and I also didn't want him, for any reason, to have his guard up. Let him think it was all going according to plan, except for some car trouble. He responded almost immediately, texting (or dictating, in his case), Any problems with my gift?

I wrote back, No problems, on ice, and that was the end of our correspondence. Poole and Kunian had last texted when Poole was leaving La Paz, hot on my trail. All their exchanges, I noted, had been terse and vague, and so I had continued in that vein.

After that, I plugged the phone back into its charger and smoked some of Venturi's weed and sipped a little more tequila. Then I turned off the lights and lay back on the bed, George and Walter beside me. I listened to the rain and watched the headlights of the cars from the street below flash across the ceiling, then disappear, then flash again.

I was enjoying the sound of the rain and the play of the lights, but I was also doing a moral calculus in my head: I needed to get Kunian off my back, *and* I wanted him to pay for his part in the death of six innocents. If he hadn't put a contract out on me, the doctor, his wife, his son, the two nurses, and Felix would all be alive.

But I didn't want to kill him.

Then I had an interesting thought: maybe I could put *him* in the trunk of a car. Was that the way forward? My new method? *Indirect* killing?

As if that didn't leave blood on my hands...

And what of Sebastian? I hadn't forgotten about that murderous bastard. Frances deserved justice and for something to be done in her name, and one way to honor her life would be to make sure Sebastian never killed again...

So he, like Kunian, needed dealing with... once I found him.

But then what? Maybe I could put them in a trunk *together*...

But I knew this was not the right path. Violence begets violence... begets —

I thought of Poole and Venturi, suffering terribly... probably dead by now...

How could I break this samsara?

9.

THE NEXT MORNING, I texted the "service" using Poole's phone, saying that I had a customer to refer. The man, thinking it was Poole, texted back and said that I (Poole) was in luck: there was a cancellation that evening and to send this referral by.

Well, it was all pretty straightforward after that. The "service" was an American who ran a U-Haul office in Tijuana but lived in San Diego and commuted every day in his company "car" — a small U-Haul van. In the back of the van, there was a false, soundproofed bottom, where one person — and, in my case, one person and two smallish animals — could lie in darkness, like in a coffin, with a tiny vent, allowing in just enough oxygen.

It seemed almost too easy to work, but because the U-Haul man crossed the border every day, he had a special commuter pass and was waved through without hassle and never looked at twice.

Of course, there was always the chance of a random search — it wasn't entirely risk-free; nothing is — and the U-Haul man's fee to act as an illicit ferryman was five thousand dollars, not the twenty-five K that Poole had told Kunian, which wasn't surprising: he'd been trying to gouge Kunian.

But the savings for me was good on two levels: I could keep some of the cash from the money belt for operating expenses, and the rest I could send to Felix's widow in La Paz, which was no compensation for what she and her daughters had lost, but I had to do something.

I would also see how much I could get out of Poole's and Venturi's bank accounts and send that to her as well...

*   *   *

In the back of his office, the U-Haul man — a midthirties fellow named Nick, a weight lifter, who looked like he was on steroids — had checked to see if I was wearing a wire but did it halfheartedly. He could tell by looking at me that I was too authentically screwed-up and tattered to be undercover, and he very kindly only charged an extra two hundred bucks for the additional passengers: George and Walter.

But that was the only nice thing about him. He had all the personality of one of his tumorous biceps: he hardly spoke and wouldn't make eye contact. He didn't seem like a lawbreaker, per se, but I figured he had become an illegal ferryman to pay for whatever it was he was injecting.

We crossed that night after he closed the shop — the trip took about ninety minutes, all told, but seemed much longer — and it was very unpleasant in the coffin-like compartment: the claustrophobia, combined with the anxiety of being discovered at the border. But this was nothing compared to what I had done to the two hit men, and I figured it was just a small taste of the karma I was sure to reap for my cruelty.

Luckily, George and Walter, used to burrowing, were seemingly unbothered by being in the compartment, which I was grateful for, and when the van finally stopped moving, around 7:30 by the glowing dial of my watch, I was immensely relieved.

But when Nick unlatched the hidden compartment and let us out of the van, it was pouring rain and we were in an empty abandoned lot in the warehouse district of San Diego, chosen, most likely, for its lack of cameras and relative privacy.

It was expected that I would get an Uber after being dropped off, but the rain was really coming down and there was nothing to stand under. George was shivering immediately, and Walter was getting wet in his mesh bag, which he didn't like at all. Nick, unsympathetic, said, "That's it. End of the road," and he slammed the van doors closed and went around to the front without bothering to say goodbye. I called after him, "You wouldn't happen to have an old umbrella, would you?"

But he didn't answer, got in his van, and drove off.

And just like that I was back in the States, though it wasn't the happiest welcome home. It was dark, and the pouring rain was drenching and cold, and there was simply nowhere to hide: all around us were metal warehouses with razor-wire fences.

There were, at least, a few streetlamps, glowing weakly, and two blocks from the empty lot I found an out-of-the-way bus stop for us to take shelter in. By then we were completely soaked, and using Venturi's phone, I got us an Uber to the Santa Fe Depot, San Diego's main train station, which was once quite grand and beautiful. But the powers that be had let it decay — it was a Spanish Colonial hall, built at the end of the nineteenth century — and if a building could have feelings, this one seemed sad.

We caught the 8:55 Surfliner to LA, due in just before midnight.

I snagged us a window seat on the upper deck of the two-tier car, and it was strange to be surrounded by so many Americans again. The border was just a few miles away, but in this brief passage from the third world to the first, I could tangibly feel the rise in median income, along with a greater societal aloofness. Eye contact was minimal. People seemed guarded, cold.

A few people still wore masks and almost everyone was hunched over their phone, intent and insatiable, which meant not much had changed, in that regard, since I had left: the phones were still in charge.

Then, right at 8:55, the train lurched into motion. Walter was in my lap, in his pink beach purse, and George was at my feet, tethered by his leash. He was sniffing for food crumbs, but then he jumped onto my lap, not wanting Walter to have me all to himself, and I made room for him. He smelled of wet dog, which was delicious, and I stared out the window for much of the trip, hoping to see the ocean, which was the big draw of the Surfliner.

But it was too dark out and rainy, and I couldn't see much at all, really, except the reflection of my own shadowy, water-streaked face. Which, as I studied it, was still somewhat new to me, just three years old, and I thought that if I saw any of my old friends back in LA, I'd have to warn them: *I don't look like me anymore...*

*   *   *

At Union Station, which was still quite grand, but also a little sad, like its cousin down in San Diego, we got a cab, a yellow Prius, and I told the driver, "Beachwood Canyon, Gower exit, off the 101, and then I'll direct you."

The driver, an older Black man, nodded his confirmation and piloted the car away from the station.

The 101 was a rainy mess, but all around us, on both sides of the freeway, was the great megalopolis: a misty sprawl suffused with the glow of several million lights.

The driver took Gower, as instructed, and a mile up Beachwood Canyon Drive, I had him turn left onto my dead-end street, Glen Alder, and my heart actually started racing, excited to be back after so long, though, of course, no one would be waiting for us.

At the end of the block, we got out of the taxi in front of my garage, which is right on the street, a separate structure. The house itself wasn't visible, especially at night: it's up a forested slope, hidden by several magnificent trees, and to get to the house from the street, there are thirteen steps to an old wooden fence and gate, and then beyond the gate are another thirty-two steps, about the equivalent of a two-story walk-up.

As we climbed the wet stairs in the utter darkness, George pulling on his leash, it was like passing through a rain forest; everything was wet and dripping, and then at the top of the steps, there it was, my little Spanish cottage, tucked into the hill like a white tooth.

I opened the door and the lights worked. I loosed George from his leash, and he began dashing about like a madman, hunting old smells and new smells. After that, I unzipped Walter's purse, and he stepped out of the bag like royalty descending from a carriage, and I said, though he couldn't hear me, "This is your new home, Walter."

10.

THE WHOLE PLACE WAS incredibly dusty and stale, like a diorama of a past life, in a museum that had been closed for a long time, but there wasn't a rat infestation, and the roof hadn't collapsed; nothing bad like that.

I went into each room, reacquainting myself with my own house, and it was like slipping into an old pair of broken-down shoes, and I do mean broken-down. The wooden floors are warped, the white-painted walls are actually yellow, and there are just four small rooms: two on the ground floor, two on the second floor, plus a bathroom, and everything is furnished with pieces I have found on the street, except for the bed, which I bought on sale at Macy's back in 2007.

It did feel luxurious, though, to have my very own flush toilet, as well as a bathtub, and, after three years of cold showers at Vic's, that night I took my first hot bath of the 2020s.

Indulging myself, I lolled in the water for quite a while, with the lights off. Then, feeling nice and clean, I swapped out the dusty sheets and blankets from my bed for the dusty sheets and blankets from the cupboard. George and Walter didn't care one way or the other, and they happily assumed their usual positions and passed out almost immediately.

But I wasn't ready to sleep just yet, and from my bedside table I picked up a Buddhist text, hoping for some shard of wisdom on what I should do about Kunian and Sebastian. It was all well and good to be home with my flush toilet and bathtub, but tomorrow the hunt for the two men would begin, and I needed guidance.

The book was called *Eight Verses for Training the Mind* — I had been reading it back in January of 2020, before fleeing LA. I turned to a random page, like the book was a Magic 8 Ball, and it was crazy what I struck upon:

> *The teachings tell us that we shouldn't abandon many for the sake of one but that for the sake of many, one may have to be sacrificed. This is illustrated by one of the stories of the Buddha's past lives...He was a ship's captain with many passengers on board...A pirate captured the ship and was going to kill all the passengers, so in order to protect the pirate from doing something that would bring...terrible future suffering, the captain killed him.*

Now, this was something to work with. I could rationalize and justify what needed to be done. I would take on the role of the captain — the Buddha! — and Sebastian and Kunian would be the pirates. Sebastian had probably hurt or killed other women besides Frances and would most likely do so again, and Kunian, as a drug dealer and pimp, was also a killer of innocents.

Executing them would still be my samsara, my nightmare, but it was also now my purpose. I was going to be an instrument of retribution and karmic justice, which would stop them from hurting others in the future. I could almost convince myself it was a noble path.

For the sake of many, one may have to be sacrificed.

And in this case, *two*. Two had to be sacrificed. By me.

But first I had to find them.

PART IV

1.

IN THE MORNING, I took George and walked up the street to the Beachwood Market, a throwback little grocery, owned by the same family for seventy-odd years, and picked up kitty litter, pet food, and coffee.

On the way back to the house, George was happy to be in his old stomping grounds, sniffing for traces of dog urine like his life depended on it. And for each sniff, he left his own message, letting the neighborhood know that he was back and wouldn't be taking shit from anybody should they pass each other on the street.

Then, as we headed up Glen Alder, the sun, after a night of rain, suddenly emerged, and the light was glorious, like a prism had been wiped clean.

We climbed the stairs to my gate, and on the other side of the fence, I said hello to everyone, all the flora and fauna, which I always do when I come home, and the whole place was high on chlorophyll and photosynthesis. The bougainvillea bushes, creeping up the hill, had gone especially mad, forming a thirty-foot carpet of the most radiant purple flowers, and the numerous trees were bright green and still dripping wet after a night's soaking.

Towering over everything, to the right of the house, like the god of the slope, was the giant eucalyptus tree, a truly mythic figure, at least a hundred feet tall and probably a hundred years old.

It was all a sylvan paradise in the middle of Hollywood, my own little forest, and George and I marched up the thirty-odd stairs to the front door.

Once inside, I set up Walter's kitty litter in a plastic pan and made some coffee.

Then it was right back out into the day. To begin my murderous hunt for Sebastian and Kunian, I needed two things: a phone and a car. In that order.

* * *

From Beachwood, I walked down to a Verizon store on Hollywood Boulevard. I had kept my cell phone number alive — had paid a minimum monthly fee for three years — but the phone itself had died a few months back.

So I got a new phone, paid for with cash from Poole's money belt, and this gave me access to my contacts again.

I left the store and pulled up the number of an old friend, Claude Brax. We had been cops together back in the '90s, and after he retired, Claude had opened a bodyguard service, which he was still running. Part of his operation has always been a small fleet of retired police vehicles, detective class — black Mercury Marquises, tricked out with tinted windows and side lamps — and I was hoping Claude could lend me one. I tapped his number, and after several rings I left a voice mail, apologizing for going off the radar for a few years, and could he call me back?

After doing that, I decided to walk a mile down to Vermont, where I still had a small office, half a block from the Dresden Bar. I still had my key, and while I was in Mexico, I'd been in touch over email with my landlord, Phil Murrin, who had kindly suspended my rent for three years, partly because of COVID, but also because the building, which is old and falling apart, is mostly a tax write-off and Mr. Murrin likes to lose money on it.

On top of that, nobody else in their right mind would rent my office: it's long and narrow and makes you feel like you're having a strange dream where the world's proportions are all off. Originally, it had been one side of a storeroom that had been cut in half to make two offices, but the architect had screwed up, and it's less like an office and more like a gangplank with aspirations to be a walk-in closet.

Anyway, that day, it was sunny and chilly, January in Los Angeles, and Hollywood had gotten spiffed up quite a bit since I had left town. There were no visible homeless encampments and there were at least a dozen new apartment buildings, not a single one with character or flair.

But what do I know? I'm not exactly a beacon of style, and as I walked east on Hollywood, I was back in my LA work clothes: blue-sponge sport coat, blue pullover sweater, white button-down shirt, and khaki pants. Each piece was old and coffee-stained and smelled like it had been in a closet for three years, and topping off my wardrobe was an old black watch cap, which kept my head warm.

So everything about me was the same as it used to be.

Except for my face, which I was reminded of a few minutes later when I ran into Monica, the last woman I had ever made love to, and she didn't know who I was.

2.

I HAD JUST GOTTEN a grilled-shrimp burrito at Machos Tacos, on the corner of Vermont and Hollywood, and was headed up the street to eat the burrito in my office, and I noticed an attractive Latin woman, in her early forties, approaching me.

She was wearing jeans and a thin blue ski jacket, and I thought, offhandedly, *That woman looks a lot like Monica,* and then as she got closer, I realized it *was* Monica and I couldn't breathe. When she drew even with me, she glanced in my direction, the way you might glance at anybody who has suddenly frozen on a sidewalk and is gaping at you. But then she sailed right past me and there had been no recognition in her eyes: I was just some strange, leering man with a deeply tan face, a face she didn't know in the slightest.

I went to call after her but it turned out I couldn't. No words would come from my mouth — I think I was too afraid — and she made a left onto Hollywood and disappeared from my vision.

Then I thought, *I still love her,* and I felt it, like an ice pick. Regret had been turned into a sharp blade. Then I tried to remember what it had been like to kiss her, but it was gone. Only the pain of the loss remained.

But it was a good thing we crossed paths, because I was sitting at my desk, in my dusty old office, no longer hungry for my burrito, and I thought, with frustration, *Where did I just see Monica's name?*

Then, out of the muddle, it came to me!

I had seen her name in the script Frances was reading, because Frances was going to play a character named Monica! "Monica" had been highlighted in yellow!

But what was the title of that script? It had something to do with guns and dying...

I thought if I could dredge up the name of the script, maybe I could find the writer; the script might have been registered in some way. I knew that writers did that — at least the ones I had met in bars who were paranoid about getting ripped off. Frances had said the writer was her friend, but I couldn't bring up at all the name on the front of the script, whom it was written by...

But the title had something to do with dying...and guns...

Trying to recall the conversation with Frances, I was pretty sure the friend was a man, who was also a director, and the title was something violent and maybe a little juvenile, which would also point to the writer being a man.

And if I found Frances's friend, maybe he — *or* she, if it *was* a woman — would know who Frances had gone to Mexico with. Maybe Frances had told the person Sebastian's last name, and if I had his last name, I could find him and put my hands on him. He would be back in Los Angeles by now.

From my desk drawer, I took out one of my old yellow pads and a pen, and I started writing down *guns, dying, death, firearms, guns, bullets, mortality*... Then I started doodling strange shapes, followed by strange faces, tormented men with crazy eyes and big noses, my old doodling go-to, and while I doodled, my subconscious was working, and the title bubbled up to the surface: *Target Practice for Dying.*

I was sure of it.

I wrote it down on the pad, and it gave me chills seeing the words written out; made me flash to holding the script and Frances being alive, four days ago, sitting next to me by that pool, overlooking the Sea of Cortez...that poor, beautiful girl...I almost started crying...

But I shut that feeling down fast.

I was going to find her killer and...and...and—
Make sure he never killed again.

* * *

On my new phone, I googled *target practice for dying.*

And what came up were horrible stories of gun violence as well as several strange articles about shooting as a way to euthanize one's pets, specifically cats. Which made me think of Walter, and I wondered what he and George were up to. Then I googled *target practice for dying screenplay.*

And that elicited countless how-to articles about "shooting scripts."

This modern detective work was going nowhere fast, but then I searched for *where do screenwriters register scripts?*

That was a bit more fruitful, and the main answer was the Writers Guild of America West, located right here in Los Angeles. I then called the number listed and got an outgoing message that informed me, essentially, that everyone was still working remotely, so go ahead and leave a voice mail or visit the website.

But the website wasn't very helpful: there was no sort of registry I could search, and in fact it said, under the FAQ section, that the only people who could access a registered screenplay were the screenplay writers themselves, which meant the whole thing was designed for copyright protection and nothing else.

For a moment, I was stumped. Then I created a fake Yahoo Mail account for a man named Walter George and wrote the Writers Guild the following note:

To Whom It May Concern at the Writers Guild of America West,

I came across a screenplay that was absolutely brilliant and I would like to locate the writer, but, unfortunately, the title page went missing while I was traveling, and I don't recall the writer's name, though I remember the intriguing title: "Target Practice for Dying."

I'm an independent producer and very interested in this film, so if the script is registered with the WGAW, could you pass on my email to the writer or send me a way to contact them?

All the best,
Walter George

P.S. I can also be reached at this number: (310) 747-5250.

I wasn't holding my breath that I would get any kind of helpful response, especially if anyone tried to search for Walter George, but it was worth a shot. Then I did some more googling to see if there was anything yet about a murder on the East Cape of a young Englishwoman, first name Frances, but there was still nothing, or at least nothing I could find with my limited skills.

So, looking for a lead in another direction, I began searching rental properties on the East Cape, and on the website of a San José del Cabo realtor, Agencia Los Cabos, I found, almost immediately, the listing for the Rock House, replete with beautiful pictures of the beach where I had spent three years swimming. There were also interior shots of the house, which was like looking at crime scene photos but without evidence of the crime: there was the couch, all pristine and white, where I had last seen Frances, naked and dead.

Disturbed by the pictures, the ones on the website and the ones in my head, I put the phone down and swiveled in my desk chair and looked out the window. My office is on the second floor, facing the alley behind the building, and I stared out at the sky and thought about that day: how we had snorkeled together and how she had trusted me and held my hand.

Then I did this Buddhist thing called tonglen, which means "to exchange" and which you can do for the living *or* the dead, and so I pictured Frances in my mind, and I breathed in the pain of her whole life, the terror that must have been there at the end and all the confusion and longing before that, and when I exhaled, I sent her love. It was like a prayer. Maybe it would reach her.

I swiveled back to my desk and decided to call the realtor — the number was posted on the website — and see if I got lucky. It was a little after one p.m. and a lot of Mexican businesses close during the siesta hour, but on the fifth ring, a woman answered: "¿Hola? Agencia Los Cabos."

I had made my cell phone private, and I said, in my bad and simplistic Spanish, "Hola, mi nombre es Walter George y soy detective de homicidios del Departamento de Policía de Los Ángeles. ¿Habla inglés?"

There was a pause and then the woman said, tentatively, with concern, "Yes, I speak English. How can I help you?"

"I'm calling about the house you have listed in the East Cape, the one in the area called Dos Ballenas, described as 'Ocean Front Retreat.' A young Englishwoman named Frances was murdered there —"

There was a sharp intake of breath on the other end of the line, and the woman said, "No one was murdered! She drowned, swimming in the sea."

"Drowned?"

"Yes, the English lady drowned," she said.

"Are you sure?"

"I don't understand what this is about. You are with police?"

She was confused and suspicious, and I said, "I need the full name of the young woman who died and also the name of the party who was renting the house last week. This is an official inquiry on behalf of the Los Angeles Police Department. The renter's first name may have been Sebastian but we don't have his last name —"

There was another sharp intake of breath and the woman hung up.

Had the name "Sebastian" caused her to gasp or was she spooked in general?

I called back and she didn't answer.

It had sounded like the woman truly believed that Frances had drowned, but I didn't know why she would think that. Had there been some kind of police cover-up because the killer — *the framed killer* — had disappeared?

This was a confusing new piece of the puzzle, and I wondered if I could get to the actual owner of the house; maybe they could be conned into providing information. Agencia Los Cabos certainly wasn't going to give me the owner's name, not now, but I knew someone who could probably get it for me, my friend Rick Alvarez. I thought of him because he works in real estate and is handy with a computer, cunning even.

Also, he loves to do me favors. Years ago, I had helped his elderly father who had fallen for a coin scam, and ever since, Rick acts like he's in my debt. In fact, Rick was the one person I had been most in touch with while in Mexico: my mail had been forwarded to him, and he had even checked on the cottage once in a while, to make sure it hadn't been broken into or vandalized. So I already owed him a call, and I pulled up his name on my new phone. His came with a smiling picture of himself: dark-haired, early fifties, youthful, twinkling eyes.

"Happy!" he answered loudly, with genuine enthusiasm, and it felt strange to be greeted this way: both his use of my real name, which I was out of practice hearing, *and* the undercurrent of affection. I had forgotten how essentially warm he was, and he continued, his excitement still at a high level. "If you're calling, that means you're finally back?!"

All our communication, for three years, had been by email, and I said, "Yes, I'm back. Got in late last night. Took the train up from San Diego."

"Great! I have a ton of mail for you, though it's all junk, *and* I want to see you! When can we get together?"

I swiveled in my chair and glanced at my reflection in the window. I hadn't mentioned to Rick, over email, that I had gotten a new face. It's not the kind of thing you casually bring up, and I flashed to Monica passing me by, not knowing me in the slightest.

I said to Rick, putting things off, "Maybe later in the week, after I get settled, we can get a drink and I'll get my mail. And…and I know I just got back to town, Rick, but can you do something for me?"

"Already working a case?" he asked, eager to be of service. Rick had often helped me in the past: along with being a computer whiz, he has access, as a realtor, to databases that can be very useful during an investigation. Luckily, I never feel like I'm burdening him with my requests; he finds case work thrilling, a nice break from chasing after a buck.

"Yeah, I'm already on a case," I said.

"What do you need me to do?"

I told him I wanted the name of the owner of a house in Mexico, in Baja, and I gave him the pertinent details. He said he had contacts in Mexico City, in the realty world, who could possibly be of help, then he asked what it was all about, and I said, being professional, "I'll tell you later."

He laughed. "Yeah, sure."

But he wasn't annoyed. In the past, he'd always asked me what I was up to when he got intel for me, and I always said, "I'll tell you later," which I never did. It was our little routine, and it had been three years since we'd bantered like this, but it came back to us naturally. Then I thanked him for looking after the house and my mail, and he kept me on the phone a bit longer than necessary, though it was kind of him to ask after George.

When we hung up, I felt I had done just about everything I could, for the time being, to find Sebastian. I simply didn't have anything else to go on. Just the screenplay and the house itself. So until I heard from the Writers Guild or Rick, I had to be patient, which meant I could turn my attention to my other problem: *Kunian.* I then took Poole's phone, which I had silenced, out of my pocket, to see if by chance Kunian had texted, and I was a little psychic, because five minutes earlier, he *had* sent a simple and direct text: ETA?

It was Tuesday, and I wrote, Should be back in the States Thursday night. Car almost ready. Bring the gift to the club?

In return, I got, within seconds, a thumbs-up emoji, then nothing else.

Which gave me forty-eight hours to figure out what to do about Kunian.

3.

EVEN THOUGH I WASN'T hungry, I ate my burrito, then walked over to Hillhurst and Franklin, to the Bank of America, where Poole and Venturi had accounts.

I could have gone to any ATM, but it seemed silly to have the dead men pay fees, and I figured I'd empty out their savings in eight-hundred-dollar increments, which is the most you can extract each day, with the idea of eventually getting it all down to Felix's wife in La Paz.

From the money belt, I already planned to give her most of the cash, keeping a little for myself to help me get back on my feet, but I was disappointed to see, once I fed the machine their cards, that neither Poole nor Venturi was very flush: Poole had a balance of roughly eleven thousand bucks and Venturi had around eight thousand.

I figured the hit man business wasn't thriving, but then it occurred to me that since they invariably got paid in cash, they wouldn't have put the money in the bank, because that might involve declaring to the government that they killed people for a living. So they probably had a stash somewhere, and that would most likely be where they lived. Which was Riverside. And that's where Kunian's club was. Which meant I now had two reasons to go to that nasty town: look for money and take a peek at Kunian and scout his security.

I just needed a car to get there, and the gods were looking after me, because after I left the ATM, with sixteen hundred dollars in my wallet, Claude Brax called me. He was in Palm Springs on business, and after some initial chitchat, I asked him if I could borrow one of his vehicles for a few days. He generously said that wasn't a problem: three of the cars weren't being used and business was slow.

I didn't tell him that my license was expired, which was why I couldn't rent a car, and he didn't ask. Eventually, I'd have to go to Motor Vehicle, but I had more important things to do. I had two men to *sacrifice,* and if I survived the ordeal myself, then I'd get a new license.

* * *

Using Poole's phone, I took an Uber to Claude's office on Olympic, near Century City. He shares a two-story brick building with an ambulance-chasing law firm, and his company is on the second floor. I climbed the stairs and his receptionist gave me the keys, told me which car to grab, and I went around to the back.

There, lined up in a row, making it look like the parking lot of a precinct, were the three old detective vehicles, all of them painted black with tinted windows and equipped with large side lamps for throwing spotlights on perps. Claude likes the old police cars, which he buys at auction, because if his company is hired to guard a celebrity's residence, let's say, he has one of his men sit in a Mercury in front of the domicile, and the detective-class vehicle signals, to the average thief or stalker, that there is police presence, which makes for a good deterrent.

In fact, before COVID, I had worked a few times for Claude when, at the last second, he needed a body in a car on the graveyard shift in front of some Beverly Hills or Bel Air mansion, and for me, it was always an easy thirty bucks an hour. From midnight to eight a.m., I'd sit in the car, drink coffee, and read — I've always been a big reader, since childhood — and almost nothing ever happened. Actually, the half dozen times I worked for Claude, nothing did happen.

So I pointed the car I took, a 2006 Mercury, in the direction of home — I needed to walk George before heading out to Riverside — and halfway back to Beachwood Canyon, a bad feeling started up in my stomach. A real bad feeling.

And I knew, with that first jab of pain inside, what this was: a reverse case of Montezuma's. My stomach wasn't used to American bacteria, even though it was a burrito that had poisoned me, and I floored the Mercury, hoping to make it home in time.

But it was a terrible mistake to not stop at a gas station or a McDonald's — I stupidly and skittishly wanted to be on my own toilet — and that last stretch up Beachwood Canyon Drive, that last mile and a half, was absolute torture.

I was desperate not to make a mess in Claude's car, and about two blocks before my street, I thought for sure I was going to lose it. But then I found one more internal gear, one more lockdown mechanism, like a sailor swinging shut one of those iron doors in a submarine after it's been hit by a torpedo and is taking on water. But that internal action could have gone either way! It could have resulted in a total valve opening, the risk had been that great, and I pulled into my garage, recklessly, at high speed, nearly crashing into the back wall.

Then I began hobbling up all forty-five steps, hoping not to lose it right before salvation, and the gigantic eucalyptus tree, godlike, was looking down on me, poor little incontinent human, and I kept thinking, *Please let this not be my karma, please let this not be my karma, please let this not be my karma.*

I made it into the house, whipped off my jacket, with George hurling himself at me, and I shouted, "Out of the fucking way, George!" and I staggered up the stairs, got my pants down, collapsed onto the toilet, and flashed in my mind to Los Alamos, 1945.

When the nightmare was over, I sat there for a few minutes, emotionally depleted.

I had barely made it.

It was the incontinence equivalent of a near-death experience, and I was rattled. How was I to go about being an instrument of retribution and karmic justice when I was ready to be fitted for a diaper?

* * *

After a hot shower, I lay down for a little while to regain my strength, then took George for a walk. His digestion was doing better than mine, and when we got back, I found some old weed in a kitchen drawer and rolled a few joints for the drive to Riverside and to help settle my stomach. I'm not fancy when it comes to cannabis — it can be old and dry, like this was — but the truth is, I don't really notice much change no matter what I smoke. I'm like a wet-brain alky but with weed.

Tempting fate, after my harrowing experience, I stopped at Tang's Donuts on Franklin to get a coffee. Instead of Buddhism, I decided to apply Christian Science, and I told myself my stomach would be fine and not to worry about it, that it could handle coffee.

It was 3:30, not quite rush hour, but, according to Waze, it would take at least two hours to get to Riverside, fifty miles to the east on the brutal 10, and I very much needed the caffeine for the long ride.

I also purchased a Mega Millions lottery ticket. If I won, I'd split the money with Felix's wife, but I didn't expect to win. For years, I've been buying the Mega Millions at Tang's, and when you scan your ticket a few days later, the little electronic reader always says: NOT A WINNER. It's like the lousiest fortune cookie ever, but I sort of delight in it every time, maybe because it feels like it's my dad talking to me, and, in my own way, I still miss him, even his put-downs.

So he comes to me through that machine. *Not a winner.* I hear it in his voice.

4.

SURE ENOUGH, THE TRAFFIC was grotesque, and it took the expected two hours to get to Riverside. I've never liked that town.

It's got a population of about three hundred thousand people, but it's stuck between at least four major highways, with thousands of trucks rumbling through it or over it every day, en route to Los Angeles, and the hot desert air is always sick with pollution. You can rarely see the surrounding mountains, and with its countless fast-food signs along the freeways, the place is like one big truck stop, with all the beauty of a truck stop.

But I shouldn't judge. It's just a town, formed by the dollar. It never had a chance.

Halfway there, around 4:30 in the afternoon, it began to pour torrentially, and the Mercury handled the road well. According to the radio, this rainstorm was one of those modern atmospheric rivers, unprecedented in fact, and as it turned out, it wouldn't stop raining for the next thirty-six hours straight, resulting in horrific floods, mudslides, and quite a few deaths, three of which I would witness firsthand.

The address I had put into Waze was for Poole's house, and Venturi's was just a block away in the same tract development. My wipers were working hard, and I could see in the rainy early evening gloom that all the houses had the same design. Probably built in the fifties, they were single-story ranches with a big living room window and a short driveway that led to an attached garage. Some of the houses had the garage on the right and some had it on the left. That was the only difference.

The whole development, called College Estates, was a thing of circles, looping around one another, and the streets were all named after eastern schools: Poole lived on Dartmouth Street, and Venturi was on Cornell. But there any resemblance to the Ivy Leagues ended. What had once been a middle-class Levittown dream had turned sour long ago. The houses looked uncared for, bitter, and the trees that lined the streets were morose and ill: the rain had come too late. Soon the whole thing would probably be torn down and replaced with condos. Or just torn down.

Dartmouth Street had a slight incline to it, and as I drove past Poole's house, which was on the right, I glanced over. There were no lights on and no car in the driveway. Playing it safe, I kept going, looped around, and came back up Dartmouth.

I then parked a little down the hill, at a good angle for keeping an eye on things, and the rain was beating down on the car like a rivet gun. It was just about fully dark now, but there was a streetlamp in front of Poole's house, which helped, and I wondered if there might be a car in the garage. There were still no lights shining through the front window of the house and no exterior lights were on, but there was the possibility that someone could be in the back of the house, just like there could be a car in the garage.

So I figured I'd wait a little while, to see if someone came home or if any lights were turned on. From what I had gleaned from Poole's text messages, it didn't seem like he lived with anyone or even had many friends, but it was better to err on the side of caution before I broke into the place, and I settled in for a little stakeout. There was still some cold coffee left, which I sipped, and I lit a joint.

In my jacket pocket was my lockpick and my extendable steel baton, which I had taken with me in case I ran into any trouble. After a while, I took the baton out and tapped it into the palm of my hand, like a violent metronome, and it helped pass the time.

* * *

Around 6:30, I figured I had waited long enough, without seeing any sign of life coming from the house, and I chose a slight lull in the rain and scrambled up the street.

But the water was flowing at nearly ankle level, and I got pretty wet. Then at Poole's door, with the rain starting to come down harder and being blown sideways by the wind, I fumbled with the lockpick, but, luckily, no one drove by, and both neighbors' houses were dark: no one home.

Finally, I got the lock to tumble and went into his place, which had a foul stink to it, like the house had bad breath. The curtains were closed over the front window, but I didn't want to put any lights on. So I used my cell phone like a flashlight and looked around. Poole's sparse furniture was worse than mine, greasy and battered, and the walls were empty: no art, no photographs, nothing of a personal nature.

But there were several closets filled with all sorts of crap — old clothes, old shoes, plastic bags containing plastic bags, a dozen George Foreman grills still in their boxes, who knows why — and I started going through the closets, looking for the money. After the closets, I tossed nearly the whole house pretty fast but hadn't yet found what I was looking for, and then my Christian Science petered out, and I had to dash for the bath-room.

Except I didn't like the idea of sitting on the dead man's toilet seat, so I took precious seconds to put paper down, like I was in an airport or a bus station, and of course as I sat down two of the pieces floated off, and I didn't have a choice but to make contact.

When I was done, I was feeling extra neurotic and really wanted to take another shower, even in Poole's grimy tub, which had a ring of pond scum. Not surprisingly, though, I couldn't find any clean towels — I rechecked every nasty closet and cupboard — which led me to open the inner door to the garage, the one room I hadn't tossed yet. It was empty, no car, but it had a work area and a washer and dryer, and on top of the dryer, there were two folded towels, which looked gray but clean. A miracle.

I went to get one of the towels and noticed that the dryer was just slightly uneven with the wall and that there were small scratch marks on the concrete floor. So I pulled the dryer out farther, and there was a wooden panel close to the ground, screwed into the drywall. I got a Phillips-head from the work area, unscrewed the panel, and there it was, tucked into a hole in the wall: a white plastic bag filled with cash, blocks of it, rubber-banded together.

I felt a little giddy, brought my booty into the house, took a shower, and left.

At Venturi's house, which was just as mean and ugly, I went right to the garage. He had the same setup behind the dryer. But with his bag of money, there were also two matching snub-nosed .38s, loaded, which I decided to hold on to. I was probably going to need them, and I didn't have any guns of my own.

Back in the car, the rain still coming down hard, I counted what I had found for Felix's widow: between the two stashes, there was a little over a hundred grand total. Which was not bad at all. In Mexico that might actually last a little while. Then I hid the money and the guns in the well of the trunk, under the spare tire, and headed for Kunian's strip club.

5.

ON THE WAY THERE, feeling wobbly stomach-wise, I stopped at a little Chinese restaurant in a strip mall, the kind that's mostly for takeout, and I ordered a big bowl of white rice to stopper me. The place had two small tables, and I sat at the table in the window and shoveled the white paste into my mouth with chopsticks. Outside, the rain was coming down in sheets. The parking lot wasn't quite flooded yet, but it might be soon.

After I inhaled the rice, I was a little steadier on my feet, and at the 7-Eleven next to the Chinese restaurant, I bought a cheap compact umbrella and a pint of cherry-flavored Pepto-Bismol. I drank half the Pepto, about four times the recommended dose, and I thought it tasted pretty good.

Fortified in this way, I drove over to Kunian's place, which was on a busy six-lane road of industrial supply stores, gas stations, and fast-food restaurants. The club itself was a windowless rectangular structure, painted black, and was wedged between an auto-repair shop and a lawn supply business called Riverside Gardens.

There was no parking on the street and the lot for the strip club was in the back of the building. But my vehicle was a little too noticeable, so I stashed the Mercury behind the gardening place, next to a dumpster and a ladder, which was leaning against the store. It looked like the ladder had been left there for a reason: maybe the roof had a leak with all this rain.

Between where I stashed the car and the strip club parking lot was a concrete wall, so I walked back out to the road, using my new umbrella. When I hit the street, the club was to the right. Above its entrance, in big letters, was DIAMOND DANCERS in red neon, along with a red neon silhouette of the female form.

I walked quickly over to the club — cars were zipping by fast, splashing water like speedboats — and pulled open the metal door. This led to a shadowy vestibule vibrating with music, and in the corner, a good-size bouncer sat on a stool behind a lectern. He was bent over his phone and didn't bother to look up.

Straight ahead was a glass door, which gave me a glimpse into the club's interior, and I slipped the baton into the folds of the umbrella as I closed it. Then I stepped up to the large man, who was wearing a black T-shirt and a black sport coat. He looked up from his phone, gracing me with his attention, and said, "Twenty-dollar cover. Two-drink minimum."

"How is it in there?" I said, handing him the money.

"Whatta you think?" He nodded toward the street and the rain, which we could hear on the other side of the metal door. "It's dead. You'll have the place to yourself."

Then he gave me a phony smile and didn't make a move to come around from behind the lectern and frisk me, which meant it hadn't been necessary to hide the baton, but I was playing it smart — a lot of strip clubs frisk their customers for weapons — and I went through the glass door.

The music got even louder and the club was as shadowy as the vestibule. There were maybe half a dozen patrons sitting in the gloom.

I slipped the baton out of the umbrella and back into my pocket. To my immediate left was a dimly lit hallway with curtained doors, which probably led to small rooms for private dances, and in front of me was the elevated stage. It gave off most of the light in the room and was long and narrow, like a models' runway, with a pole on either end.

A stripper, naked, with long black hair, was swinging around the pole on the left, the one closest to me; she was holding on to it sideways with one arm and one bent knee. She was twirling at a real high speed, like a gymnast or something out of Cirque du Soleil, and her hair, a black whip, was beautiful.

Two men were at the table in front of her, folded dollar bills poised in their hands, and the rest of the men were spread out among the other front-row seats, which were right up against the stage, so you could be really close to the girls, close enough to touch.

Behind this front row were tables for your more shy types, of which there were none this evening, and to my immediate right was the bar. It came with padded high chairs and a hulking bartender bent over his phone, which seemed to be a theme.

He was wearing a black T-shirt and black sport coat, the same uniform as the bouncer, and in addition to the stripper on the stage, there were two strippers in bathing suits working the room: one was trying to get a man in the front row to buy her a drink, and one was sitting at the bar, waiting. Waiting for me.

I went to a shy-person table in the middle of the club, and she popped right over, teetering on her high heels, eager to make a buck on a slow night. She was a redhead, wearing a white one-piece bathing suit, which seemed odd: strippers usually wore bikinis, like the stripper who was working the other men in the room. But maybe the one-piece made her different and that could be a good thing in a place like this, something to set you apart.

She sat down next to me and didn't waste any time: "Buy me a drink?"

"Sure," I said, and looked at her closely: she was late twenties, a natural flame-top, freckled all over, and a little too skinny. Drug skinny. She wore a lot of makeup, but somehow it couldn't hide the black rings under her eyes, which were mostly pupil with a little bit of blue.

But she smiled wide when I said I'd get her a drink, and I was glad to see that her teeth looked all right, they weren't meth teeth, and she made a motion to the waitress, a Mexican girl in the shadows, who was also bent over her phone — the whole world was — but then she saw the redhead out of the corner of her eye and hustled over. The redhead said to me, "Okay if I get a champagne? It's sixteen bucks."

"Sure."

"Champagne," she said to the waitress, who barely looked twenty-one, and the waitress nodded at the champagne order, then said to me, "What do you want to drink, sir?"

I thought about it a second, then remembered that old wives' tale about beer being good for your stomach, something about the hops, and I ordered a Heineken.

"Bottle or frosted glass?"

"Glass," I said, and the waitress left.

The redhead put her hand on my arm. "Thanks for getting me a drink."

"I'm happy to," I said.

"I'm Carly."

She then sat up real straight, affecting a good posture, and offered me her hand. She was smiling and playacting a formality, and I thought of Frances: how *she* had offered me her hand to shake on the beach, and suddenly I was back there in Mexico, standing by the sea with her.

Then I came back to the present, shook the living girl's hand, and said, "I'm Lou."

"Where'd you get the tan, Lou?"

I almost said Mexico but thought better of it. It was brazen enough to be in the club, though I didn't think Kunian, if he made an appearance, would ever recognize me. The man he had seen on FaceTime had a wild beard and long hair and the lighting hadn't been too good; plus, it was FaceTime: a small image on a cell phone. Now I was shaved, wearing a black watch cap, and sitting in a dark bar: he would never know me, and on top of that, it would never occur to him that I'd walk right into his club like this.

And my old face? The one he might remember? Well, that was long gone.

But I didn't have to announce to this stripper that I had gotten my tan in Mexico. I didn't have to be *that* brazen, and I told her I'd been in Hawaii for a month, fishing.

"Nice," she said. Then she squeezed my arm and made a sound. "Does fishing make you strong? I can tell you're built. I like older guys with big shoulders. I have daddy issues."

She smiled coquettishly when she said that; it was a line she used — her whole act was a line, a real old one, despite her youth — but before I could respond, our drinks came and I paid for them, gave the waitress a nice tip. Carly watched me closely, tried to catch a glimpse of my billfold. When the waitress left, we clinked glasses and drank, then she said, touching my arm again, "You want a private dance?"

I said, "Let's slow down a little. Talk first. Then maybe a dance," and I took out my wallet again, peeled off a twenty of dead-man money, and put that on the table. She smiled and made the bill disappear into the little purse she carried. "What you wanna talk about?"

I sipped some more beer and felt like it was sitting well on top of the Pepto, and drinking the beer gave me a second to come up with my angle. Then I said, "I'm looking for a job. I work security. You know, bouncer, doorman, whatever's needed, and I was wondering what this place was like. They hiring? You could give me the inside scoop."

"You want to work *here*?" she said with disbelief. "This shithole?"

"*You* work here."

"That's because I have to."

"Why's that?"

"It's a long story."

I nodded. Didn't want to press her too hard. I said, "So you really think I shouldn't try to get a job here? Could be easy money for me. Security probably doesn't have to deal with the bullshit you have to put up with."

"That's true. Better to be a bouncer here than a dancer. You get treated better."

"Oh, yeah? What's the boss like? It's Kunian, right?"

I thought there had been a good opening, but I'd gone too quickly. She was guarded now. She said, her tone flat, "You know Kunian?"

"I know him by reputation."

She looked at me over her champagne glass, then finished her drink, making fast work of it. Everything she did was fast. "Buy me another?"

"You get a cut on the drinks sold?"

"Not much, but, yeah, you know how it works."

I nodded and signaled to the waitress.

"Another champagne," I said when she came over, and on the stage, the stripper with the long black hair had just finished her dance and was squatting in her high heels, scooping up the few crumpled dollars that had been thrown at her feet. Then from the hallway, near the entrance, a new girl appeared. The bartender, who was also the DJ, announced, "Please welcome our next sexy diamond dancer, Alexis!"

The whole thing was worn-out Kabuki, tired and clichéd, but everybody was making an effort to play their part on a rainy night: the strippers, the bartender-DJ, the men with their folded dollar bills.

I said to Carly, still pushing things, "Kunian here now? Maybe I could talk to him about a job."

"You don't want to talk to that guy."

"Why not?"

Her drink came and she put down half of it in one long gulp. Her pupils were extremely dilated and not because the room was dark. I wondered what she was on. I said, "Why don't I want to talk to Kunian?"

"Are you a narc or something?"

"No. Far from it. I'm a pothead. I'm stoned right now."

She looked at me and laughed. Then she said, working me as much as I was working her: "Buy a dance, and I'll tell you why you shouldn't talk to Kunian. Plus, in the room, nobody can hear what I say." Nobody could hear us now with the pounding music, but she wasn't stupid: if she was going to gossip about her boss, privacy would be better.

"How much is a dance?"

"Fifteen minutes is seventy-five. Half hour is one-fifty. Plus…" She smiled, put her hand on my leg.

"I'll do the half hour," I said. "But you don't have to worry about, you know, the *plus.*"

"Oh, sure," she said, and she stood up, took my hand, and led me over to the bar, proud that she had landed a fish and landed one fast. I was still holding on to my beer, and the bartender, who was built like a refrigerator, a block of fat and muscle, came over to us, and she said to him, "We're gonna have a half hour dance, Stevie."

Stevie, whose jet-black hair was slick with some kind of gel, maybe motor oil, didn't say anything, just nodded: he would put us on the clock, and when the half hour was up, he'd come get her or send the bouncer to get her.

That business taken care of, she led me to the hallway, which had three curtained doorways running down the left side, and I could see that at the end, the hallway turned to the left and to the right, like the letter *T,* and to the left were the dressing rooms and bathrooms and to the right was a door marked PRIVATE.

For our dance, Carly chose the middle curtain, a heavy velvet thing, which she pushed aside, leading us into a small chamber, lit like a photographer's darkroom: it had an ambient red light. In the dimness, I made out a couch-like banquette against the wall, and next to the banquette was a small table with a box of tissues. Not a good sign.

She closed the curtain and said, "Sit down."

Obedient, I did what she said, lowered myself onto the banquette, but first I made sure I wasn't sitting down on anything offensive. Thumping music from the bar was piped into the room, and she said, "You gotta pay up front."

I put my glass of beer by the upsetting tissue box, took out my wallet, and handed her two hundred bucks. "Keep the extra fifty," I said.

Smiling in the red-hued glow, she put the money in her purse and took off her heels. Without them she was suddenly quite small, maybe five foot three, and she started undulating in front of me, getting right to it.

She wasn't without appeal, and I could feel my heart quickening, but I was here for other reasons. I took her by the hand and guided her to sit next to me. She looked at me quizzically, and I said, "I really just want to talk."

"About Kunian?"

"Yeah," I said. "I'm serious about getting a job here. And it's good to know what the boss is like."

"I don't think you're a narc, but you're lying," she said. "No way you're throwing all this money around because you want a job. But give me another hundred and I'll tell you anything you want."

I dropped the pretense and gave her another hundred. "Is he here tonight?"

"Yes."

"Is he in the room marked 'Private'?"

"Yes."

"Is he alone in there?"

"He's never alone."

"Why not? He's got security in there?"

"Yeah. Stevie's older brother is in there. His older, meaner brother. But Kunian also has two slaves."

"*Slaves?*"

She nodded, sort of excited. I could see she wanted to gossip. She said, "The cartel cut off his hands, but they gave him two slaves to help him. They wipe his ass. Everything."

"How do you know they're slaves?"

"That's what everyone says. It's a husband and wife from China. They don't speak English; they never look you in the eye. Anyway, that's what Stevie says, they're real slaves, and he would know. He says the cartel sells people left and right."

Then, already bored with the topic, she took a little baggie and a straw out of her purse.

"What's that?"

"Nothing hard. Just coke. Want some? Want to party?"

I shook my head no — I was still thinking about Kunian and his slaves — and she shrugged, put the straw, which was cut in half, into the baggie, and snorted up a nice bump. Then she switched nostrils, and when she was done, she shook her whole body playfully, pretending to be like a dog ruffling its coat. As an encore, she licked the straw, ran her tongue over her gums, and put the baggie away.

After that, she stood up and started dancing again, more for herself than for me.

Then she reached back into her purse, took out a vape pen, and pulled on it. As she danced, the white smoke wrapped around her like fog.

I said, "What's your split with Kunian on this?"

"Seventy-thirty," she said, rotating her hips, and talking fast because of the coke. "And he gets the seventy. But he throws in baggies of blow or whatever you want, as a way to keep a hold on you. Only problem is four girls OD'd the last six months on fentanyl. So now we call stripping here working the slab instead of working the pole. Get it? Like the slab in the morgue. But that's why I only snort coke. That *isn't* cut with fentanyl. And smoke weed."

She held out the vape pen as an example of weed and offered it to me, but, showing rare restraint, I shook my head no. She said, "Don't you want to party at all? You tipped me good. And we've got like twenty-five minutes left."

"Why don't you get out of this place?"

As soon as I said it, I regretted it. It was as much a cliché as her come-on in the bar had been. But I had lost control of the conversation, of my would-be interrogation — I couldn't help but feel protective — and she stopped dancing, put her hands on her hips.

"Oh, God, are you giving me the speech? Like why-is-a-nice-girl-like-you-a-stripper-so-why-don't-you-come-home-with-me-and-give-me-a-blow-job?"

Then she laughed and started dancing again, not really upset; she had too good a buzz.

"That's not what I'm saying," I protested, though it sort of was, except for the blow-job part. "But it sounds like you hate this place, and you could at least work somewhere else. Like at a club where the girls aren't overdosing all the time."

"Yeah, but no other place will take me."

"Why not?"

I needed to stop playing social worker and get back to Kunian, but I couldn't control myself, and rather than answer me, she stopped dancing again and peeled down her one-piece bathing suit all the way to her ankles and stepped out of it.

She didn't have any pubic hair, but there was a piercing, and by her freckled right hipbone was a thick purple scar, about four inches long.

Now I understood why she didn't wear a bikini. She ran her finger over the scar and said, "This is why I'm stuck here. I had to get a cesarean because of HPV, you know about that? Anyway, the doctor did a shit job and fucked me over. Nobody wants to see something like this. But before the scar I used to be in the top places. When I was nineteen, I was at the Seventh Veil in Hollywood. You know it?" She wiped her nose with her finger, then ran the coke residue along her gums.

"I know the Veil."

"Yeah, it was big-time. Because of my freckles, I have the girl-next-door look" — she did a little coked-up spin for me, displaying her whole naked form, including her white buttocks, which *didn't* have freckles — "and when you have that, you don't have to spend money on fake tits and shit. You make good money no matter what, and I was making like a thousand a night there. Ten-hour shift, but still. That was good money. Maybe we were there at the same time. Maybe you saw me."

"I doubt it. I was there a long time ago." When I was a cop, we pulled a lot of runaways out of the Veil, tried to send them back home.

"Well, they'd never take me now because of this." She ran her finger back over the scar. "I'm done as a stripper. Wrecked. Only this shithole will have me."

Then she sat back down next to me, naked, completely uninhibited with her body, as she had been the whole time, and it was the opposite of erotic, which was a good thing. Made us just two people sitting in a red-lit room, one dressed, one not dressed, and she took out her baggie of coke, did another bump, and licked the straw again like it was covered in sugar. Then she put the baggie away and lifted her skinny arms into the air, stretching with coked-up delight. I studied her for a moment and her breasts were small and bud-like, but with unusually large, distended nipples.

She caught me looking and said, "I got big nips because I breast-fed my daughter for like two years. And don't worry, no coke for two years. I was good. But that's another reason why I'm stuck in this dump. My daughter. I'm a single mom, no child support. So I gotta make money and I don't have any skills. I wanted to go into makeup, maybe work in the movies and TV, that was my plan when I was at the Veil, but I think I'm probably too old now."

"How old are you?"

"Twenty-six. Do you think that's too old? I think it's too old to go to school for makeup."

"That's not too old at all."

She looked down at the floor, young and uncertain. Innocent even.

Then she said, "Want me to dance some more, or you want to keep talking?"

"Let's keep talking."

"If you're not a narc, why you so interested in Kunian? Are you gonna get me in trouble?"

The conversation was back on track, and I tried a new angle. "No, I'm not going to do anything to get you in trouble. I work for some people that he owes money to, and they wanted me to get a feel for the situation here."

"Really?" She was intrigued by this, and her jaw was starting to swivel from the coke. "What are you, a bookie or something?"

"Sort of. And my boss wants to know how tough Kunian is. And you said he's got only one man working security in the office. Stevie's older brother. Which seems light for a drug operation. And that's what this is, right? Not just a strip club. You said the cartel gave him the slaves."

I knew, of course, from Poole, that Kunian still distributed for the Jaliscos.

"Yeah, a lot of shit runs through here," she said. "Like if you wanted blow, I'm supposed to hook you up, have you talk to Stevie. But you can get anything here. Heroin. Speed. Big Pharma."

"So why's the security so light? Just a guy up front and a guy in the back."

"And Stevie. He's got a gun and a baseball bat behind the bar. But we don't need a lot here. Everybody in Riverside knows this is a cartel club. So nobody makes trouble. Not even the cops. But that's because they're paid off. The cartel is bigger than the government around here."

"Who told you the cops are paid off? Stevie?"

"Yeah. So what?" Then she really started working her jaw, and I could see her tongue under her lip, wriggling like a worm, searching for coke, for sensation.

"Is Stevie your boyfriend?"

"Sometimes. But I make him pay for it."

Then, suddenly, her jaw was going *real* fast and a weird look came over her face, like she'd had some terrible insight. Then her head tilted way back and her eyelids were fluttering. Alarmed, I said, "You okay?"

At the sound of my voice, she snapped her head back, like someone trying to wake up while driving a car, and she looked at me as if she didn't know me, but then, all of a sudden, she was in my lap, wrapping her arms around my neck and hiding her face in my chest.

I could smell her overly sweet perfume and a hint of oniony sweat, and I gently tried to lift her off — her skin felt clammy — but she was stubborn. She held on tight, her face now buried in my neck, and she pleaded, in a whispery voice, "Please, just hold me a second. The coke's got me feeling weird. It happens sometimes. I'm really cold and scared."

She started trembling bad — not faking it; she was like someone with hypothermia — and so I held her, thinking I was going to have to call 911, but after a while, the trembling passed, and she got off my lap and lay down on the couch, curling herself up into a ball. She was just a tiny thing, really, could fit on half a couch, and she closed her eyes and put the tip of her thumb into her mouth. I stood up and draped her bathing suit over her, a meager blanket. Then I added my jacket, and she whispered, her eyes still closed, "Thank you. I'll be better in a few minutes."

"Okay," I said, and picked up my beer off the table and leaned against the wall. From that angle, I could see that underneath the couch, left behind by other men, were crumpled tissues, looking like sickly white mushrooms, the kind that grow only where it's dark.

The minutes passed, and I sipped my beer and kept watch over Carly, playing nurse, and I wondered how long she had for this world. Then, without disturbing her, I got a joint out of my jacket pocket and lit up. I didn't think she would mind.

6.

A LITTLE WHILE LATER, back in the bar, Carly was doing much better. On my suggestion, she'd had a big glass of pineapple juice (canned) with ice, which got her back to normal. Normal being wasted but not having to go to the ER, and she was working the room again, trying to sell a dance, and a few more men had shown up.

I was back at the same shy-person table in the middle, taking my time with a second Heineken, and my plan was to wait for Kunian to leave, then follow him back to his place.

Here at the club, he had three men, all of them probably armed, but at home, he was sure to be more vulnerable. After he went to bed, I'd slip into his house, put Venturi's .38 against his forehead, and kill him in his sleep. Like putting an animal down.

He wouldn't even know he was dead.

Only I was having second thoughts about doing it. I felt myself losing my nerve. When I had taken lives in the past, it had always been in self-defense, which was nightmare enough. But this was something else; this was execution work.

Then I thought, *Maybe I don't have to kill him. He doesn't really know this new face; still doesn't know my name. I could just walk out of here.*

Sure, I'd be looking over my shoulder the rest of my life — he had found me once — but maybe that was *my karma:* to live in fear. And he *would* continue to hunt me. Because of me he had lost everything. Three years ago, he was living on a yacht in Marina del Rey and now he was in a dead-end strip club in Riverside. Trapped. A slave himself to the Jaliscos, and if he tried to steal his way out, this time they'd cut off his head. So they owned him, kept him around as a cautionary tale to their other crews, and he couldn't hurt them for what they had done, which had put the target on *my* back. It was classic projection. He needed a scapegoat to satisfy his rage.

But I couldn't go through with killing him — I was no executioner — and I took another sip of my beer, just about ready to leave. I looked for Carly, wanting to signal goodbye to her. She was sitting with a man at a table in the front row, and I caught her eye, but she looked away, like she was ashamed. Then two men were suddenly on either side of me, digging iron fingers into my arms, pulling me to my feet.

One of the men was Stevie, the big bartender, and the other guy, just as big, must have been his older brother, the one Carly had mentioned. Stevie said, "Let's move it, asshole," and they started perp-walking me toward the hallway with the curtained doors.

"What's going on?" I said, acting the fool, but they didn't answer, and I looked over at Carly again, and she lifted her drink to me with an apologetic shrug to her shoulders. She was letting me know she was just playing by the rules of the game, which were to look after yourself, and I didn't fault her at all. Of course she had told her boyfriend Stevie I had been asking about Kunian — I was an idiot to have stuck around — and as the two brothers got me to the hallway, I said again, "What's going on? I don't understand."

"Shut up," said Stevie, and his breath in my face was rancid, sour. I tried then to shake myself loose, but it wasn't happening. Stevie and his brother were large boys, strip club muscle, and we went down the hallway, then through the door marked PRIVATE, and there he was, Jack Kunian, sitting in his office, like an old spider, waiting for me.

He was behind a big wooden desk, and in the far left corner of the room, sitting at a table, was his Chinese couple. They looked to be in their fifties, but a hard-labor fifties, and Kunian, who was in his midsixties now and didn't seem to recognize me at all, said, "Who the fuck are you? You told one of my girls I owe a bookie money? What is this shit?"

I said, "That was just a story I was telling to impress the girl. I thought she was cute."

Kunian stared at me like I was crazy and lying, both of which were true, and he certainly was no longer the obese kingpin of three years ago. His body had withered, probably from the trauma of his torture — he wore a dark blazer that hung on him loosely — but even in his shrunken state, he still radiated a profound malevolence. His thyroidal eyes were bugged out and bloodshot, full of hate, and his big head was bald and liver-spotted. I noticed that the top half of his left ear was missing, which was new, and on the desk in front of him his arms rested unnaturally. Sticking out of the sleeves of the jacket were two flesh-colored prosthetic hands that looked like mannequin hands, meant for appearance, not function.

He said, "A fucking story? About a bookie? You're full of shit. What's your name?"

It was astounding: he really didn't recognize me at all. Not as the man he had seen on FaceTime four days ago *or* the man who had stolen sixty thousand dollars from him back in 2020. Sixty thousand bucks that I had spent on a new face and three years of hermitdom and Buddhist study, none of which was doing me any good at that moment. I said, "My name is Walter George. I was just flirting with the girl, bullshitting, that's all."

"Check his ID," said Kunian, like an order, and Stevie's brother shoved his hand inside my jacket and came out with my wallet. Poole's and Venturi's bank cards were, thankfully, in my side pocket, and my wallet didn't have any identification. I wasn't carrying my expired license or my bank card, which had also expired. But inside the wallet *was* a badge from the LAPD. It wasn't mine, but one I flashed sometimes to get in doors that might be closed, and the name on it was Shelton, my old friend who died back in 2019.

While his brother inspected the wallet, Stevie kept his hands dug into my right arm, and it was in my right-hand pocket that I had my baton, which made it harder to get at, him holding on to me like that, but it was doable. Except the time wasn't right yet. If I tried to get the baton now, it would be too much of a struggle. I had to wait for some kind of advantage. The brother said to Kunian, "There's nothing in here except a badge, LAPD, last name Shelton," and he tossed the wallet onto the desk in front of Kunian and grabbed my left arm again.

Kunian said, "Aang, come here," and the Chinese man right away got up, came over to the desk, and held the wallet for Kunian, showed him the badge and all the cash. Kunian looked up at me. "You're a cop from LA? What the fuck are you doing here?"

"Came for the dancers on a rainy night, try to cheer myself up."

"Who you working for?"

"I don't work for anybody. I wanted to look at pretty girls."

Kunian said to the brothers, "Did you assholes check if he's carrying? He's a fucking cop, he's probably got a piece."

Stevie's brother scowled and stepped in front of me, and I thought maybe this was my chance. As he frisked me, I could kick him in the balls, then take out Stevie.

But before I could put this plan into action, the brother unloaded a right uppercut into my stomach, lifting me off my feet. That was his warm-up before patting me down, which I wasn't expecting, but it was a good thing, in a way, because I hadn't set myself for it, and I vomited out a mixture of rice, beer, and Pepto-Bismol.

This caused the brother to jump back, not wanting to get sprayed, but he did get sprayed, and he said, "Oh, fuck," and Stevie, shocked and probably disgusted, let go of my arm, which was a mistake. He had muscle but not brains, and I was gasping for breath, bent over, but nevertheless, I had the presence of mind to dig out my baton, which I flicked open and swung backhanded, and it caught Stevie in the face and just about took off his nose.

The Chinese woman screamed, and Stevie's brother, covered in vomit, tackled me to the ground. Straddling me, he got in a wild punch to my neck. But that woke me up, brought me a little more to my senses, and I swung the baton, which I had managed to hold on to, and I hit him hard on the side of his head and the baton opened up a big gash in his scalp.

The baton, sixteen inches of steel, cuts like a knife, and his hands went up to his head, blood gushing, and from my prone position, I hit him again on the point of his head, like a hammer hitting a nail, and pushed him off me.

He was still conscious, but in too much pain to do anything, and as I got to my feet, Stevie, his face a mask of blood, came at me, kind of slow but trying, and I grabbed his arm and threw him hard across the room. He went flying into the table by the Chinese woman, and she hadn't stopped screaming the whole time.

But both brothers were down, and Kunian was pushed way back in his chair, frightened, and I think he recognized me now, because three years ago I had hit him with that same baton and split his ear in half. Back then, the ear had folded over like a flap but later they must have cut off the top part.

A little dizzy, I staggered toward him and grabbed my wallet, not really thinking that straight. But I didn't want to lose Lou's badge, it had sentimental value, and then the Chinese man, who was still standing next to Kunian, suddenly opened the desk drawer, took out a Glock, and fired at me at point-blank range.

But somehow he missed, and I was out the office door and running down the hallway, back into the bar, just as the bouncer from the front was coming through the glass door. He had heard the gunshot, even with the music, and I slashed at him with the baton, and he went down, and then I was out on the street.

It was still pouring, and I looked over my shoulder, but none of them were following, and so I ran to the back of the gardening place, got into the Mercury, and drove out of there fast. Drove all the way back to Los Angeles in the deluge, going forty miles an hour, barely able to see the road in front of me. But nothing could kill me that night. Not bullets. Not apocalyptic rainstorms. Not even my own stupidity.

7.

I TOOK THE GUNS and the plastic bags of cash out of my trunk and climbed the stairs to my house. It was still raining hard, and the tree branches, sodden with water, were hanging incredibly low. I had to push my way through the wet leaves, like going through the brushes of a car wash, and I wondered if the hill behind my house might shear off in a big mudslide.

I unlocked the front door and stashed the money and the guns in the kitchen, where there's a hidden panel that opens up. Behind the panel is an ironing board, like a Murphy bed — it's an original feature of the house from the 1920s — and the whole thing makes for an excellent hiding spot, which I've used before. Now it held the cash for Felix's widow and Venturi's two guns.

I dragged George out into the rain, long enough for him to do his business, and back in the house, I checked Poole's phone: Kunian had called several times but had left no voice mails, though he had sent a single text: That bastard showed up here tonight. He's a cop from LA, named Shelton. Either you betrayed me or you're dead. You better hope you're dead.

That was his cheery message, and I didn't text him back.

And on my phone, there was nothing from Rick Alvarez or the Writers Guild.

So, one day back in LA and both my cases, if you could call them that, were in terrible shape. No leads on Sebastian, and, even worse, Kunian was going to find out very soon that Lou Shelton was dead, but after doing a bit more digging he'd discover that Lou Shelton's best friend was a man named Happy Doll.

Which meant I was going to have to go back to Riverside tomorrow and kill Kunian.

No more waffling. No more screwing up.

Then I'd find Sebastian and do the same, and I flashed in my mind to Frances, her mottled neck, and that was followed by a memory of the bodies lined up in the doctor's lodge, dead because of Kunian, and I felt hatred for the two men, which I needed to fuel my violence.

I shed my rain-soaked clothes and got into bed, George and Walter beside me, and I didn't bother reading any Buddhist texts.

I just lay there in the dark and as the rain played its watery music against the window, I thought of the future. After I killed Kunian and Sebastian, I would sell the cottage and disappear from the world, causing no more harm. I'd take George and Walter, find a new Dos Ballenas, and wait for death.

That was my grim plan. Then suddenly I thought of Monica, whom I had seen on the street that day. But I quickly pushed her out of my mind. I had given up on love. I wasn't capable of it. And thinking such thoughts, listening to the rain outside, I fell asleep.

PART V

1.

In the morning, I woke up paranoid that Kunian might already be close to discovering Happy Doll, and I wanted to get out of the house with the animals. In the past, men had come hunting for me at my home, and one time they poisoned George to keep him from barking, and he nearly died. So I packed up food for the two of them, along with their bowls, and grabbed Walter's kitty litter.

For myself, I packed a small bag with a change of clothes, some weed, and Venturi's guns. I also took plenty of cash and Poole's phone, but I figured I didn't need Venturi's, so I left it behind. If I wanted to communicate with Kunian in some capacity, I'd use Poole's device. It took two trips down the steps with all our stuff, but I got us out of there: George on his leash, Walter in his pink bag from Mexico.

It was still coming down hard, and I went to La Mirage Inn, a hot-sheets motel on Franklin and Beachwood, but they were all booked up, so then I drove over to Hollywood Boulevard.

I'd always wanted to stay at the Hollywood Downtowner Motel—I like its style—but it's hard to be a tourist in your own town. So this was my chance, and even in the rain, the motel's sign was beautiful: the Vegas font, the bursting star at the top, and, in general, the place has a real retro look, but that's because it actually hasn't changed in sixty years. It was retro before it was retro, and I paid extra for an early check-in, plus the two animals, and the clerk gave us a tiny room on the second floor, overlooking the small pool. Everything was nice and clean, and I put Walter's kitty litter in the bathroom, along with their water and food bowls.

Then, in the small closet safe, I stashed Venturi's guns, and George and Walter had already made themselves at home on the queen-size bed, each taking one pillow.

I sat down on the bed with them and checked my phone. Still nothing from the Writers Guild or Rick Alvarez. I then took out Poole's phone and reread Kunian's text from the night before: That bastard showed up here tonight. He's a cop from LA, named Shelton. Either you betrayed me or you're dead. You better hope you're dead.

Maybe he still wasn't onto Happy Doll, and I wrote back, from Poole's phone, I'm not dead. Haven't betrayed you. Can't talk. But will bring you Shelton tonight. He slipped off but we have him again. You owe me 75 k.

I thought that might confuse Kunian in a good way, maybe slow down his hunt for me, and the text resulted in Kunian trying to call, but I turned off Poole's phone. I would deal with Kunian later: night was better for murder, more cover.

* * *

Perhaps because of my stomach problems the day before, I passed out for a few hours on that nice motel bed but woke up to my phone ringing, and it was Rick Alvarez, calling me with good news. Through his realty contacts in Mexico City, he had found the owner of the Rock House. I was expecting someone living in Mexico, but it was a man here in LA, a lawyer named Vincente Calderon, and Rick had done some extra digging for me.

"He's got his own firm," he said. "Calderon, Vasquez, Reynolds, and Ochoa, in the US Bank Tower, seventieth floor, two from the top. Bigtime."

"This is extremely helpful, Rick. US Bank Tower. I can find him there."

"I also got his home address. You want it? I looked up the property records. Mount Olympus. The guy is loaded."

"Yeah, give me the address."

He did, and I wrote it down, and Rick was right to assume that Calderon was well-off. Mount Olympus is a famously wealthy neighborhood that lives up to its egoistic name: it's built on a mountaintop in the Hollywood Hills, and you have to be as rich as a god to live there.

"I found something else about this guy for you," Rick said. "He's a lawyer for the cartel. He's all over the *LA Times* if you google him."

I was silent a second. How did this connect, if it did? I said, "Which cartel?"

"Sinaloa."

"Interesting," I said, thinking.

"What do you want with this guy?"

"I'll tell you when it's over."

"I know you will, Hap," he said, laughing.

We were playing our game again. I said, "I really appreciate your help with this, Rick."

"It was easy. But, hey, can you believe this rain? What's happening to the world?"

"Nothing good," I said, then Rick had another call coming through, and we said goodbye. On my phone, I quickly skimmed some articles about Calderon on the *LA Times* website. He had been a poor kid from Boyle Heights who had gone to Stanford, then UCLA Law, and it was a kind of feel-good story, except he'd ended up as a mouthpiece for the Sinaloa.

Some of the articles were accompanied by pictures of Calderon, mostly shots of him standing on the steps of the Hall of Justice downtown, and he looked vaguely familiar, but I wasn't sure why. He was a dark, handsome man, late fifties, with one of those white-lightning albino stripes in his left eyebrow. Which I've always been a fan of, and maybe that's what made him seem familiar: my bias for that kind of eyebrow.

As I read about Calderon, I wondered about all these connections to the cartels I was having: Kunian peddled for the Jalisco; the doctor had been a medico for the Sinaloa, and Diablo had been a sicario for them. Poole and

Venturi, as outside contractors, had also been in their employ. Working for the Sinaloa, they had been looking for the stripper, the coke mule, when they stumbled on the doctor, which was when he noticed that Poole had a scar like mine, everything came unraveled, and he ended up spilling about me and Diablo.

Then the Sinaloa had paid Poole and Venturi to kill the doctor and his family for their part in Diablo's death and had also put a bounty on my head. So it wasn't just Kunian who was to blame for the death of Felix and the doctor's crew; it was also the Sinaloa.

And me, of course. I was the most to blame. I was the fulcrum.

But I hadn't really considered the Sinaloa's part in all this, chiefly because there was no way to hurt them. That would be like striking out at a small country. Now here was this Sinaloa lawyer, Calderon. How did he fit in?

But the thing was, I realized, he probably didn't. Working for the cartels, whether in Mexico or here in Southern California, was like working for IBM back in the '70s: they were everywhere. Still, it was interesting, another Sinaloa connection, and either way I wanted to talk to this man. I wanted him to tell me who had rented the Rock House last week; I wanted him to give me Sebastian.

It was around 1:30 p.m., and after making my phone private, I called Calderon's firm. A receptionist answered by rattling off the four names of the firm: "Calderon, Vasquez, Reynolds, and Ochoa."

I said, when it was my turn, "Mr. Calderon, please."

"Who's calling?"

"This is Walter George with the DA."

Naturally, she didn't recognize the name and said, "I can take a message."

"Does that mean he's not in the office and is working from home?"

"I can't —" She stopped herself. What she was going to say was that she couldn't give out that kind of information, which indicated to me that he *was* working at home. She said, regaining her composure: "I can take a message. What is your phone number, Mr. George?"

"I guess that means he's home. Especially with this rain."

"I can take a message —"

I hung up then. He had to be home. Things had changed during COVID: people worked from home more often. And if he wasn't home, I'd go downtown to his office.

But before I scaled Mount Olympus, I had to walk George. The rain had stopped — the lulls were brief, barely a few minutes long — and I needed to seize the opportunity and get him outside. We strolled a few blocks, and he had a nice bowel movement, which pleased me. I like it when his stools look healthy, nicely formed, a good color. My own bowels, I disdain, but George's I study with concern and affection.

2.

I took the Mulholland Highway, and this was a mistake.

There was a steady light rain, not too heavy, but the hills above the highway, from the cumulative downpour, were shearing off. Mud and rocks, some quite large, were tumbling onto the road, which isn't a highway at all, really. It's a curving two-lane mountain pass, completely feral, which happens to overlook one of the largest megalopolises in the world: Los Angeles. Except there wasn't much to see that day. The city was shrouded in white mist and rain, and as I evaded the mudslides and rocks, I tried my best not to drive off the cliff edge or into an oncoming car.

Around three o'clock, still in one piece, I arrived at the black-gated mouth to Calderon's driveway. His house was near the top of Mount Olympus Drive, but you couldn't see the house from the road. It was up a hill, out of sight, and in front of the gate, at car-window level, there was a call box with a camera eye.

I lowered my window and pushed the required button. I could hear several rings come from the box, then a woman's voice, with a Spanish accent, said, "Yes? What do you want?"

I knew my police-looking vehicle would be visible on a screen up at the house, and I held up Lou's badge to the glass eye. I said, "I'm with Robbery Homicide, downtown, and I'd like to speak to Mr. Calderon. It's urgent."

There was a pause, then the black metal gate slowly swung open.

I drove up a curving fifty-yard incline, with ficus trees lining the drive on both sides, and at the top of the incline, the house and a circular driveway were revealed. At the center of the drive was a large fountain, still doing its thing even in the rain, and the house was a severe-looking mansion: modern gray concrete, big windows, and incongruous castle-like flourishes, turrets and such, which made it look cheap rather than expensive. There was a black Lincoln Navigator on the circular drive and to the left of the house was a stand-alone four-car garage that must have held other vehicles.

There was no lawn separating the driveway from the house, just a slate ribbon, like a moat, which was lined with giant ceramic pots of fruit trees: oranges, lemons, grapefruits. I parked the Mercury and ran, in the rain, to the enormous modern front door, which was a huge slab of wood painted black. Before I could ring the bell, a Mexican woman, midforties, wearing an actual maid's outfit, opened the door.

"Come in," the maid said with a heavy accent, and I entered.

It took a lot out of her, but she managed to close the enormous door. She turned to me, out of breath. "You are with police?" She was the person I had spoken to on the call box.

"Yes," I said, and showed her the badge again.

"Wait here," she said, pointing to a large high-backed leather chair along the wall.

Then she walked off, and I sat down. I was in a spacious high-ceilinged front hall, which, on the left, had an exposed winding staircase to an upper floor, and, straight ahead, at the end of a long hallway, which was the direction the maid had traveled, was a large living room with enormous windows that looked out onto a pool and what was probably a view of the whole city but right now was a curtain of white mist.

Then a tall blonde woman came walking down the hallway. She was in a thick white robe and Ugg slippers, and her dark-blonde hair was pulled back tight with a black band. She walked in a slightly staggering way and was carrying a glass of white wine. She appeared to be drunk. I stood up, and she smiled at me as she approached. She was in her late fifties, early sixties, and had high Scandinavian cheekbones and a lined face that was handsome, beautiful.

"How can I help you?" she asked. There was the slightest trace of an accent, maybe Swedish, and her eyes went up and down my body, and she smiled again. "Maria said you're with the police."

"Yes, my name is Lou Shelton, and I'm with Robbery Homicide." I flashed the badge and put it away. "Are you Mrs. Calderon?"

"Yes. What do you want? Maybe a glass of wine?" She was being silly, tipsy.

"I was hoping to speak to your husband, but perhaps you can help me. I'm looking into the murder of a young Englishwoman at your house in Baja."

She stepped back like she had been struck. "What are you talking about? The young woman drowned." She seemed less drunk now.

Just then Calderon himself came down the hallway, with the maid, trailing behind him, looking chagrined. Calderon was also in a white robe: neither he nor his wife had gotten dressed on the rainy day. "What's going on, Annika?" he said angrily as he approached.

"This man is with the police," said Mrs. Calderon. "He's here about the girl down in Baja." She gave him a frightened look, and he was alongside us now and he was several inches shorter than his wife, but he was as darkly handsome as his photos on the internet, and I could see that the eyelashes of his left eye, matching the stripe in his eyebrow, were also white, and, again, he looked familiar. I had known a guy in the Navy with one of those eyebrows; maybe that was the resonance.

"What is your business?" he said to me, angry, barely controlling his rage.

"I'm sorry to show up like this, Mr. Calderon, but I spoke to your realtor down in Baja, but they couldn't help me, and I'd like to know the name of the person who was renting your house last week. I'm looking into the murder of the young Englishwoman —"

"*Murder?* Who the fuck are you? Let me see some identification."

"My name's Lou Shelton." I flashed the badge and put it away.

"I need more than that," he said, and when I didn't make a move for my wallet, he said, "Get the fuck out of my house," and he looked at the maid: this was her fault, she had let me in, and the woman bowed her head. Then he pulled open the door and repeated himself: "Get the fuck out of my house, whoever you are."

His wife, holding tight to her wineglass, staggered to the leather-backed chair and sat down in a slump. I said to Calderon, "I just want a name. Of the renter. The young woman was murdered."

For a moment, he looked away, a tell, then said, "She drowned. And we're not liable. And you're not going to shake me down. Now, get the hell out of here. I'm calling the police."

He took his cell phone out of his robe pocket, and I said, "Why are you lying?"

He looked at me, his eyes flashing with anger, and he pressed 911 on his phone, put it on speaker, and I could hear it ringing. I stepped outside into the rain, and he slammed the door closed.

3.

THAT HADN'T GONE as well as I had hoped, to say the least, and I made a right out of the driveway and raced the car down Mount Olympus Drive.

A thick stream of water was running along the curb, Los Angeles was drowning, and wanting to get off this main road, which would be how the cops would come, I turned onto a side street.

My plan was to wind my way over to Laurel Canyon Drive, which would feed me into West Hollywood, where I could disappear and be harder to pick off by the police. There wasn't too much they could do to me, but impersonating a cop is never a good look, and I didn't have any proper ID.

At the intersection of Laurel Canyon and Hollywood Boulevard, I was worried that there would be a patrol car waiting for me — there were only so many ways off Mount Olympus and the Mercury was easy to spot — but when I got there, I didn't see any police vehicles. There *was* a government-looking car, though, a blue Chevy Impala, and as I turned onto Hollywood, it waited two cars, then swung in behind me.

That stretch of Hollywood Boulevard is residential, not honky-tonk, and the Impala kept a nice distance, just enough for me to wonder if maybe I *wasn't* being followed. To test things, I made a sudden and quick right onto Fairfax and the Impala turned right as well, which still could mean nothing. But I didn't think so.

Half a mile later, at Sunset, I made a dangerous left against traffic, hoping to lose the tail, if it was one, but the Impala made the left as well, though it nearly had an accident.

Which meant I was definitely being followed, and whoever was doing it didn't care anymore if I knew. But they also weren't putting on a flasher and trying to pull me over, which was actually more ominous. They wanted to follow me, then put the arm on me, but not out in the open. Calderon had clearly reached out to somebody. Somebody other than the LAPD.

I contemplated trying to lose the Impala, but I also wanted to know who was driving the car. I wasn't sure if there was one or two people in it — it was too far back to tell with the rain — and I couldn't read the plate, which was a shame. If I had the plate, I could call it in to Claude Brax: he had contacts at Motor Vehicle.

So I had a lot of questions as I drove east on Sunset: Why had Calderon lied about Baja, and whom would he call to come pick me up, driving a government-issue-looking car? Were they FBI? Would a Sinaloa lawyer have an FBI agent on his direct dial? A corrupt one, maybe?

I made a left onto Highland, subconsciously going in the direction of home, like a migratory bird, but I was really just driving, no destination in mind, while I tried to figure out what to do. Three times in the last five days, I had run from situations, like a blundering clown, and there was a real pattern here: I stick my reconstructed nose where it doesn't belong and things go wrong; it had happened at the Rock House, the strip club, and now Calderon's.

It was quite the losing streak, which was why I decided to go to Tang's Donuts and see if my lottery ticket had come in. Maybe I was due for some luck. I could also use a coffee, and at Tang's whoever was following me wouldn't make a move, but maybe I could.

4.

TANG'S SHARES A STRIP MALL with half a dozen other businesses, and I parked in front of the dry cleaner. Before entering the donut shop, I looked back at Franklin and saw the Impala drive slowly by.

I went inside and the place was empty, except for the proprietress, an older Chinese woman in a blue smock. I ordered a coffee and a plain donut, which would actually be the first thing I was going to eat all day and it was a little after four o'clock. I hadn't wanted to test my stomach, and I also hadn't been particularly hungry.

There are three tables by the front window at Tang's, and I put my coffee and donut, which was in wax paper, on the table farthest from the door. Then I went over to the lottery machine and scanned my ticket and Dad said, NOT A WINNER.

I went back to my table, sat down, and looked out the rain-streaked window. On the other side of the small parking lot, about fifteen yards away, the Impala was now parked parallel to the donut shop, right near the entrance to Franklin. This gave it easy access to the street if I tried to make a run for it in the Mercury, which I had parked vertically, its nose facing the dry cleaner.

So I'd have to back up, then try to get past them, which meant I didn't have a chance.

If I tried to run for it.

The passenger-side window of the Impala was directly across from me, and I could see that a man — white, short brown hair, midthirties — was sitting on that side of the car. He looked government issue, just like the Impala, and so I was dealing with two individuals: the man in the passenger seat and whoever was driving, and I could just about make out the shape of the driver, who looked to be a man as well.

And looking at the car, I was trying to understand Calderon: Why would he send these two after me and not the police? And why be part of a cover-up down in Baja? Was it a PR thing? Didn't want to be associated with a homicide? Maybe as a cartel lawyer, he had to be extra clean since his clients were extra dirty?

The men in the car would have answers.

I could hit them with the baton and see what they had to say.

But first I wanted to know whom they worked for, and I stepped outside, shielded from the rain by the overhang of the roof. I checked out the Impala's back license plate and memorized the numbers. The man in the passenger seat swiveled his head to look at me and we made eye contact. We were playing a funny game, and having clocked their plate, I noticed that the front plate of my car was so caked with mud that it would be impossible to read, and I wondered if that was the case with the back plate, but I didn't step out into the rain to check.

I went back inside Tang's — the old lady behind the counter didn't look up from her phone, and I thought to myself, poetically, *Once we had lives and now we have phones* — and I sat back down, took out *my* phone, and texted Claude the numbers on the Impala's plate and asked if he could run them.

Then I sent a second text: P.S. After I'm done with this case I'm working, I'll take you to Musso's as a thank-you for the car and for running the plate.

Claude, like a lot of ex-cops, loves Musso and Frank's, it's old-school, steaks and martinis and creamed spinach, and right after I sent the P.S. text I got a call from a 310 number, which is LA. I looked at the man in the

Impala, who was looking at me. Could it be him? His partner? Was I on speakerphone in the car and they had somehow gotten my number?

I answered, tentatively: "...Hello?"

"Is this Walter George?"

The man in the Impala didn't seem to be talking, he was just staring at me, but I had given that name, Walter George, to Calderon's receptionist at the law firm. But how they had gotten to my cell phone from that phony name I had no idea. Spooked, I said, "...Yes. This is Walter George. Who's this?"

"My name is Justin Kearse. I was forwarded your email. I'm the writer of *Target Practice for Dying.*"

It took me a second to understand what the hell this person on the phone was talking about. Then it came to me all at once, and, falling immediately into character, I said, not faking my enthusiasm, "Oh, my God. I'm so glad you called. I loved your script."

5.

"*REALLY?*" HE ASKED EARNESTLY.

"Yes. It was fantastic. A great read. You're very talented."

"Thank you. That's very nice of you. The Writers Guild forwarded me your email. And so you're a producer? I didn't...you're a producer?"

He sounded quite young and milquetoasty, and what he was going to say, but course corrected, was that he hadn't found anything about "Walter George the film producer" on the internet. But he was obviously curious about my interest in his script; otherwise he wouldn't have called. Though I could also hear skepticism in his voice, a concern that he was dealing with a crank of some kind, which he was.

I said, "I'm new to the producing game, but I have funding — I used to be in tech — and I'm looking to finance low-budget films." Over the years, I had drunk with a few writers at bars and had listened to them talk shop, and not a one had success. Maybe it was the bars I was in. But I had picked up enough about the business to fake it on this call, or so I hoped.

He said, "How did you get my script? I haven't really exposed it that much."

"It's a long story. But, listen, I'm very eager to speak with you. Where in Los Angeles are you?"

"I'm...I'm in Atwater."

"I'm not far from there. I'm over in Hollywood. Why don't we meet up in person and I can tell you about myself and make my pitch why you should work with me."

I was afraid if I told him, over the phone, the truth behind my inquiry, he'd hang up — he might not even know that Frances was dead. But in person, I could be more convincing, and I could get from him what I needed: the full name of the man Frances had gone to Mexico with. Either he would know it or he could direct me to a friend of Frances's who would have the information. This young man on the phone was the key to finding Sebastian.

"I'm free to meet … Friday," he said, clearly nervous that I wasn't for real.

"I was thinking today." I looked at my watch, then looked at the man in the Impala and gave him the finger, which he returned. I said, "How about happy hour at the Bigfoot Lodge? In forty-five minutes. Are you near there?" That was a bar in Atwater that I liked, then before he could answer, I said, "You should know I'm willing to pay nicely for your script. You're a writer-director, and you've made one film, correct?" I remembered that bit of information from Frances. "Now that I know your name, I realize I'm already familiar with your work. I'm sorry but I'm blanking on the title of the film, but it was excellent."

"You mean *The Woods*?"

"Yes, that's it!"

"It's on Shudder. That's where you saw it?"

I didn't know what Shudder was, but it sounded like some sort of channel, and I said, "Yes. I thought it was fantastic, very suspenseful. And scary."

I made a leap saying "suspenseful" and "scary" but the title made me think those would be good adjectives to use, plus it was playing on a channel called Shudder, and he said, sincerely, "Thank you. It was super low-budget. You know, like a lot of horror. Shot it in fifteen days. I went into debt to make it."

"Well, I thought it was great. You're like a young Hitchcock."

"Oh, man. Thank you."

He couldn't help but believe my compliments: he was desperate for them. Even from a stranger who might be a crank. I said, "So let's meet at five? Maybe we can make a movie together. And like I said, I can pay for the script. Maybe even six figures." I hoped this dangling of money would seal the deal.

But he didn't say anything. He was still skeptical. How could he not be? He was milquetoasty but not an idiot, and I was going too fast, but I had to go fast. I said, "You know what? I'm going to be at the Bigfoot Lodge at five. No matter what. If you show up, I'll be thrilled and I'll buy you a drink. I'll even buy you two drinks. I'm just a really big fan and would love to meet you."

He hesitated, then said, with an undercurrent of excitement, "All right, I'll meet you there. It's actually just a few blocks away. I guess I can walk in the rain. This is…this is great." And I could hear in his voice a shift. The shift into the deluded hope that some kind of crazy, lucky break was maybe coming his way, the kind of break everyone in Hollywood dreams about. But it's an utter mirage, of course. Those lucky breaks are about as common as buying a winning lottery ticket at Tang's.

I said, "Wonderful! See you at five, then."

"How will I know you?"

"I'm wearing a blue sport coat and black watch cap. How will I know *you*?"

"I have glasses, black frames, and sort of a thick beard."

"All right. We're on, then. See you soon, Jason. Jason, right?"

"No, Justin."

"Shit, sorry. And your last name is again —"

"Kearse. Sounds like 'curse,' but, you know, spelled different."

"Right, see you very soon. Bye now."

I hung up then before I completely blew it and looked out the window. I didn't need the men in the Impala now. I was going to meet Frances's friend Justin Kearse, which sounded like "curse," and he was going to lead me to Sebastian.

6.

I SAT THERE A moment, contemplating how to lose my tail. Then I finished my coffee and donut and exited Tang's. The rain was quiet at the moment, not too heavy, and I waved at the guys in the car, then broke into a fast jog, exited the lot, and crossed Canyon Drive.

I was headed for the Gelson's supermarket, which is right at the corner of Canyon and Franklin, and when I got to the other side of the street, I looked back and the guy I'd been having the staring contest with was slamming the Impala's door and running after me.

I ran into Gelson's — I had a good lead on the guy — and went to the housewares aisle, which always has just a few items, frying pans, baking implements, and things of that nature, and hanging from a hook, I saw what I had come in there for: a very sharp-looking paring knife.

I grabbed it, then went back to the front of the store and its half dozen registers, and my friend from the Impala was standing near the east-side entrance/exit, scanning for me and looking anxious.

By a register, I ducked behind a magazine stanchion, and he didn't spot me, but I could see him. He was wearing a rain-streaked blue windbreaker and had lifeless brown hair and lifeless bland features. He was definitely FBI or something adjacent. His partner must have stayed at the car, figuring I'd have to come back for my vehicle.

The person in front of me at the register finished paying, and I stepped forward.

I was visible now, nothing to hide behind, and I quickly paid for the knife. I removed it from its packaging — I wanted to have it ready — and then the guy saw me.

I ran out the west-side exit, and he went out the east-side one.

Knife in my jacket pocket, I dashed across the parking lot, running between parked cars, and I was headed for the exit onto Franklin. My pursuer, an angry look on his face, was hell-bent on cutting me off, moving through an adjacent row of cars, and then we were both in the open.

He was just a few yards behind me, at an angle, but I didn't think I could outrace him. So I veered toward him ever so slightly and he didn't have time to slow down — the parking lot had a little bit of a downward slope to it and was slippery from the rain — and at the last second he understood what was going to happen and I saw panic in his eyes. He was probably around five nine, 150, and I'm six two, 190, and I ran right through him, like I was Jim Brown, and I didn't look back, but I heard his body hit the pavement.

I then left the Gelson's lot the way I had come in, and as I crossed Canyon, I saw that the other man from the Impala was crouching at the back of my car, wiping mud off the license plate. I took out the paring knife to get it ready, and just then he turned and saw me, and I ran to the Impala and jabbed the knife deep into its front right tire and yanked it out. I could hear the tire exhale, like an animal that's been gored, and the guy who had been squatting by my car was now running at me in the rain.

I dropped the knife in my pocket, took out the baton, and charged him, the baton held up in the air like a cavalryman's sword. Scared, he skidded to a stop and so I gave him the same treatment as his partner — he was built about the same — and I just plowed right through him. I heard his body hit the ground, and then I was in the Mercury, pulling out of the lot fast and onto Franklin.

In my rearview mirror, I saw the guy I had just flattened get up, and then I drove past the other one, who was limping out of the Gelson's lot. I waved goodbye to him and made a left onto Bronson. It was 4:30. It would take me roughly twenty minutes to get to Atwater Village. Which was perfect. I didn't want to be late for my Hollywood meeting.

7.

THE BIGFOOT LODGE IS all wood-paneled and wood-beamed, like a ski or hunting lodge, and has a huge banner on one wall that says: SASQUATCH NATIONAL FOREST. It's done up like a real national parks sign, the font and the design, and I guess the place is supposed to be tongue-in-cheek, but it's been around forever and actually does seem like a lodge. Which is why I like it: you feel as if you're in the mountains somewhere, but outside is Atwater Village, a little bedroom community adjacent to Glendale.

There's a front entrance to the bar off Los Feliz Boulevard, and a back entrance off the parking lot. I parked in the back and ordered a drink from the bartender, a skinny young woman with tattoos, piercings, and black eyeliner, like a goth biker. She looked to be all of twenty-five and seemed very world-weary, and I didn't blame her. Pandemics, atmospheric rivers, mass extinctions, grotesque inequities, the false and manipulated division of the country into Eloi and Morlocks. It must be hard to be a young person these days and keep your chin up. I'm in my fifties and forget about the chin: I'm bent at the waist from the strain of it all.

The place was utterly empty—it had just opened—and I took my drink, a Don Julio on the rocks, to one of the booths along the back wall. I didn't expect Justin to be on time—no one ever is—and I pulled out my phone and Claude had just texted me: the license plate I had asked him to run belonged to a car that was part of the DEA motor pool. So those guys were, as I suspected, federal agents, doing dirty work for a Sinaloa lawyer, which made sense from the perspective of the cartel: if you're bringing drugs across the border, it's good to have the people who are supposed to stop you, like the DEA, on the payroll.

I texted Claude back: Thank you.

Then I quickly googled Justin Kearse — saw his cherubic bearded face and thick black glasses — and there weren't many entries, but I clicked on a blog review of *The Woods,* hoping to get a sense of the movie if I had to bullshit more, and what I gleaned was that the film was about a serial killer, a man, who manipulates people into committing murder, so that, in the end, he has two victims: (1) the killer, who he makes sure is caught and is sent to prison for life, and (2) the actual murder victim. Meanwhile, the serial killer never gets caught because he never commits a crime. It was a disturbing premise, and the blog gave the film three and a half stars. As I finished the article, Claude called me.

I answered by saying: "Thanks for running that plate."

"No problem, but listen, I just got a funny call. Somebody ran *your* plate. A prick from the DEA. Guy named Phil Xavier. Tried to push me around. Wanted to know who was driving the vehicle and I asked him why."

"What did he say?"

"Said he had a confrontation with the driver but didn't get an ID. So I told him the car was stolen this morning and I hadn't called it in yet, which he didn't believe. Anyway, I don't want to know what's going on — this way I don't have to lie to anyone — but everything okay, more or less? The guy sounded pissed."

"All good. I appreciate you covering for me, Claude."

"You know I've got your back, Hap. We go back almost thirty years," he said, which made me smile. Not too many people actually like me, let alone have my back, and then I saw Justin Kearse come in the front entrance. While he closed his umbrella, he was scanning the bar, looking for me, and I caught his eye and waved at him. I then held up my index finger, indicating *Give me one minute,* which was a nice touch on my part, I thought, would make me look more Hollywood, and I said to Claude, "I have to go, pal. I'm at this bar and somebody just showed up I have to talk to. But thanks for everything, and we'll go to Musso's soon."

"Sounds good. Stay dry. And don't kill anybody with the car. That's all I ask."

"Not with the car," I said, and hung up. Then I got out of the booth and walked over to the young filmmaker, extending my hand. "Justin!" I blurted, hale-fellow-well-met and all that, and we shook hands, which was a little awkward. His hand was a small, damp thing that got swallowed up in my big paw, and he was a tiny fellow, in general, mostly beard and a little potbelly, and I said, "Thanks for meeting me in the rain."

"It's crazy out there," he said. "Coming down really hard right now."

"Well, let's get you a drink and warm you up. We have a lot to talk about."

8.

ONCE I HAD JUSTIN situated in the booth, a whisky in front of him, I took out five hundred bucks of dead-man money and slid it over. It was a creepy thing to do, but I wanted to pull the Band-Aid off this situation and get to the truth. Now that he was here, I didn't feel like futzing about, discussing a script I hadn't read or a movie I hadn't seen, and I figured five hundred bucks would make my deception a little easier for him to take.

He looked at the money but didn't touch it. He thought something erotic was afoot and said nervously, "What's that for?"

"Nothing weird. Don't worry. But I'm not actually a movie producer, Justin. That money is for meeting with me. For talking to me."

"Oh, shit. What's this about? I knew this was —" He cut himself off, and I saw him eye the door, like maybe he'd make a break for it.

"I want to talk to you about your friend Frances. The actress. The English girl. You told her she could have the role of Monica in your movie."

His eyes behind his glasses were now very afraid. "Why are you asking me about Frances?"

I could tell he had heard something. I said, "You know she's dead, right?"

"I saw something Monday. On Facebook." He stared at me, confused and frightened. "This is crazy. Why did you lie to me? Why did you bring me here?" He looked at the door again, but he was afraid to run for it: I must have seemed like a giant to him.

I said, "I just want to ask you a few questions about Frances."

I then took the money and put it in the chest pocket of the red flannel shirt he was wearing. He watched me do this: on one hand it was five hundred bucks, which is a nice amount, and on the other hand a very strange and large man was being intimate with his person and shoving money into his pocket.

I said, "What did you read on Facebook?"

He looked at the door again, like it might save him. He wrote horror movies but was scared of life. I said, "I'm not going to bite. What did you read on Facebook?"

He looked at me, a little wild-eyed, and said, "Her best friend posted that she had drowned down in Mexico. But why am I here?" His hand touched the money in his pocket but didn't take it out. It was a subconscious tell. He wanted the money. He added, "How do you know Frances?"

"I met her down in Mexico. And she didn't drown. She was murdered. Do you know who she went to Mexico with?"

"Murdered? What are you talking about? This is crazy." He started sliding out of the booth, and I put my hand on his arm and squeezed him so he felt it.

"Don't leave," I said. "Just answer a few questions, make five hundred bucks, and then you can go."

I released his arm. He wasn't going to move now. He was too frightened.

I said, "Are you going to be cool?"

"... Yes."

"Good. Now, tell me: Do you know who Frances went to Mexico with? Do you know his last name? His first name is Sebastian."

My knowing that name caused a change in his eyes: I suddenly wasn't completely nuts.

He then said, a bit more trusting, "Yeah, that's who she went with. Some guy named Sebastian."

"How do you know this?"

"She texted me the night before she was going, like one a.m. Said she was bringing my script with her to Mexico, and she sent a link to a music video this Sebastian guy had produced, like maybe he could produce our movie. But I didn't get her text till the morning, and by then she had already left."

"What's his last name?"

"I have to check my phone. I don't remember it. It was more than a week ago. And…and I still can't believe she's dead. Why did you say she was murdered?"

"Just get out your phone. Find her text message," I said urgently. I was close now.

He dug in his pocket, got his phone out, then started scrolling through his messages. "That's weird. It's not here."

"What do you mean?"

"I can't find a recent text from her. But I looked that guy up after I watched the video. And…and he's bad news. She never should have gone with him. That's what I would have told her, but I got her text too late."

"Why was he bad news? And do you have the link to the video? We could get his name that way."

Then something occurred to him. "I know why there isn't a text. It was a DM on Instagram." He then opened up his Instagram, started looking for the message, and I said, "Why did you think he was bad news?"

He looked up from his phone. "Because he raped some girl in college, but then got off because she died in a car accident before they went to trial. It was on the second page of his search. Frances must not have looked past the first page."

Then he glanced down at his phone. "Found her message," he said. "His name is Sebastian Calderon. That's who she went to Mexico with."

I nodded. Should have figured that one out sooner.

But now I knew why Vincente Calderon had been so familiar to me.

He looked like his son.

9.

A LITTLE WHILE LATER, I left the bar by the back exit.

It was dark out and raining pretty hard, and I hovered a moment beneath the overhang of the roof. I was building up the courage to make the dash across the lot to the Mercury, but then I noticed a car, parked parallel to the back door, that looked just like the Impala. But I knew that it couldn't be.

Except it was, because then I sensed something or someone behind me, and I turned around and the two DEA agents were oozing out of the shadows, their guns pointed at me in the rain. The agent who had chased me into Gelson's said, "Get in the car. The back seat. We want to talk to you."

"Talk about what? How much Calderon pays you?"

He thrust his gun at me. "Shut up. Turn around and keep your hands out of your pockets. Walk to the car."

"Are you Xavier?"

The way the other guy looked at him, I knew I was right. But Xavier didn't give anything away, just waved his gun and said, like a threat, "Turn around and walk to the car."

I faced forward like he told me, and Xavier was behind me on my right, and the other one was behind me on my left, both of them about two feet back. I took a few steps toward the car, getting rained on, and I wondered how I could play this. If I reached for the baton, they might be trigger-happy and shoot me. So I figured I'd make my move in the Impala, in close quarters, and the one on my left, a real gentleman, opened the back door of the car for me.

I was to slide in, followed by Xavier, his gun on me the whole time, but just before I lowered myself into the vehicle, a car pulled into the lot and put all three of us in its headlights.

I sensed the two agents stiffen, caught off guard, and I swung my right hand back in a chopping motion and got Xavier in the throat.

He immediately dropped his gun, his hands going to his neck, and I slammed the door shut and turned to face the other one. His gun was on me, but we were still in the headlights, and the driver of the car, witnessing the violence and seeing the guns, began to honk, repeatedly, hysterically.

Lucky for me, the agent had the good sense not to shoot me in front of a witness, and I took out my baton and chopped him on the side of the head. He went down, and I turned back around, and Xavier was choking, lying on the ground now, still holding his neck, but I didn't think he would die.

The person behind the wheel stopped honking, but I couldn't see them — their headlights were in my eyes — and I gave them a blind wave of thanks.

Then I stabbed the back left tire of the Impala with the paring knife and ran over to the Mercury. I fumbled with the keys — it didn't have a modern fob, and my hands were shaking from adrenaline and nerves — but, eventually, I managed to get in the machine, drove it around the car of the Good Samaritan, and floored it out of there.

A few miles away, at the Arco on Hillhurst and Los Feliz, I parked next to the air pump. Lying on my back, in the rain, using my cell phone as a flashlight, I found the small GPS tracker on the inside lip of the rear bumper. I stood up and smashed it under my foot. I flashed to the guy cleaning my license plate back at the parking lot in front of Tang's. That must have been when he planted it.

Since I was at the Arco, I filled the tank, and in the mini-mart, which had a number of diverse items, I got a package of disposable white latex gloves, a carryover from the pandemic, and I also got a new umbrella since I had left my other one at the strip club. Then I was back in the car, heading for the Downtowner, so I could walk George in the rain. On the way there, I called Rick Alvarez: I needed his help again. For years, Rick has paid for high-quality search engines that tell him what he needs to know about potential real estate clients — their arrests, bankruptcies, addresses, shoe sizes, you name it — and what I wanted him to find out was where Sebastian Calderon, son of Vincente Calderon, lived. I just hoped it wasn't with his father on Mount Olympus, because I didn't think I could get into that fortress-like mansion a second time.

Rick picked up after a few rings, and I gave him Sebastian's full name and asked him to find his address. He said he'd call back with the information in fifteen minutes: he was just finishing up an early dinner with his wife. I thanked him and hung up. At a stoplight, I turned on Poole's phone but there was nothing from Kunian. I almost felt like I was neglecting him.

I put the radio on and the DJ on 88.5 said the rain should stop around three a.m. and that there had been half a dozen deaths so far due to flooding, mudslides, and general chaos. But it wasn't so bad that we were being told to stay home. We were free to drive around and possibly get ourselves killed, which was already on my agenda, as it were, so no change in plans was necessary.

I parked the car in the Downtowner lot, and as I walked through the door of the motel room, with George jumping all over me, Rick called back. He had found what I wanted. Sebastian Calderon lived in Penthouse B of the El Royale apartment building, over on the edge of Hancock Park. "Another nice address," said Rick. "Almost as nice as Mount Olympus. Clark Gable lived at the El Royale."

"I didn't know that," I said.

"Oh, yeah, a lot of stars lived there. So what's this all about?"

"I'll tell you later."

10.

I took a hot bath and smoked a joint in the tub, figuring the steam would dissipate the weed smell, and as I lolled there, I replayed the events of the day, not without regret. I kicked myself for not seeing the Calderon connection sooner, but I had been caught up in the myth of the Rock House as it was down in Dos Ballenas: that the owners never used it. And maybe until Sebastian showed up last week, that had been the case...

Well, it was all working out anyway.

I knew where Sebastian lived and was going to pay him a visit.

And the bath felt good. Was doing its job. Restoring me for the busy night ahead.

After my bath, I got into dry clothes and snuggled a little with George and Walter, savoring the one good thing in my life: loving those two guys. Which also felt worrisome. I thought: *What if I don't make it back tonight? Who will look after them?*

I knew that Rick couldn't take them: his wife was allergic to cats and dogs and a lot of other things. And my friends who used to dog-sit George, an older gay couple, Rafi and Manuel, had both died during the first wave of COVID.

Then I thought of Monica. She had always liked George, and I was sure she would like Walter. Impetuously, I called her, after not speaking to her for more than three years, and she answered.

"Happy, I can't believe you're calling. It's so weird."

"I...why is it weird?"

"Because I thought I saw you yesterday. It was like that thing where you think you see someone on the street, but it's not them. But it's like a premonition because then you turn the corner and there they are. And now here you are calling. And it's been, I don't know, years."

I didn't want to tell her that yesterday hadn't been a premonition — she *had* seen me — and I glanced at my new face in the motel mirror.

I said, "Yeah, it's been a long time since we last talked. I...I was in Mexico for a while."

She was silent now. The rush of my calling had passed, and the strangeness was back. The strangeness and hurt feelings that had driven us apart years before. But she rallied and said, "So how are you?"

"I'm...I'm fine," I said, and the utter absurdity of calling her out of the blue and asking her to look after George and Walter, if something should happen to me, was driven home. And it became clear to me why I had really called: in case I died later that night, trying to kill Sebastian and Kunian, I wanted to hear her voice one more time. I said, "And how are you? Life all right?"

She hesitated, then said, "I'm actually at work, Happy. I'm bartending at the Dresden again, and I'm...well, I'm in the bathroom, on a quick break, and I have to get back. I left Billy by himself, and it's actually crowded, even with the rain. But why don't you come in later and have a drink?"

That's how we had met years before: I had been one of her barflies at the Dresden. I said, "I can't tonight, but some night soon, okay?"

"That would be nice," she said. "Well, I have to go, Hap. It's so weird that you called."

"Yeah."

"But I'm glad that you did...Bye now."

"Bye," I said, and I almost added, *I love you,* but I didn't. I wasn't that insane, though I did feel very strange after we hung up, and I tried to identify what the feeling was, and it hit me: it was hope of some kind.

Then I took a piece of paper off the Downtowner Motel pad that was on the side table by the bed, and I folded it in half and wrote on the front: *Manager.* Then on the inside of the paper, I left a kind of will and testament, stating that Monica Santos was to be contacted to come get the dog and the cat in the event that I did not return to the room.

I included her phone number and signed it *H. Doll,* instead of my full name, so it wouldn't seem like a joke, and I also put a hundred-dollar bill with the note, to help ensure that my wishes would be followed.

* * *

After that, I went over to Thai Town, a few blocks away, and had a bowl of fish-ball soup at Ganda Restaurant. I needed fuel for the night ahead, and in my right-hand pocket, easy to reach, I was now carrying one of Venturi's .38s, fully loaded. It was nestled next to my baton, which made that my weapons pocket. My other pocket was for tools: lockpick, paring knife, latex gloves, lighter, and two joints I had rolled, in case of an emergency. In my inside pocket, I had Poole's phone and my wallet, which was freshly stuffed with cash for any contingencies that might arise. Like bribes. Or flat tires. Who knows what.

So I was set for the night. A one-man army.

While I ate my soup, I did a search on my phone and read up on Sebastian's college case: he'd been a senior on the swim team at Stanford, and two months before graduation, April 2010, he was arrested and charged with rape. He had drugged the girl, whom he had been out with on a date, but she came to while he was strangling her. Which must have been his thing: it's how he had killed Frances.

Following his arrest, he was released almost immediately on bail, and a year later, right before the trial, as Justin Kearse had recounted, the young woman, the victim, died in a single-vehicle car accident, and without her testimony, the DA was forced to drop the charges. The car accident had happened late at night, in Half Moon Bay, south of San Francisco. With no witnesses. The autopsy revealed that she was drunk and on pills.

Then there was nothing more on the internet — the story faded out — and I wondered if Vincente Calderon, with his connections, had freed his son by engineering the young woman's death and making it look like an accident. And had he done something similar, in a way, down in Dos Ballenas? Turned a murder into an accidental death, a drowning?

It was plausible, and I thought it might have played out like this: the East Cape police — the ones who had arrived at the house — had seen through Sebastian's setup. Even though I had run, it had been a crude frame. So they go to arrest him, but daddy, with his Sinaloa connections, swoops in, pays them off, and it's declared a drowning. Sebastian walks free again.

As a theory, it made sense, but Sebastian would fill in the gaps or tell me where I was wrong, and after I finished my soup, I headed for the El Royale to have a talk with him. And maybe I was getting fancy — *or* I was still scared of killing someone in cold blood — but I had a new idea for how I could make sure Sebastian never hurt anyone again. I'd get him to confess. To Frances's murder. And maybe to involvement with the murder of the young woman in Half Moon Bay, if my hunch was correct. Then I would let the authorities take care of him. *And* his father. That was the new plan.

But if it didn't work, I had the .38. I could still play the ship captain to Sebastian's pirate.

Then I would go to Riverside and play the ship captain again.

11.

THE EL ROYALE IS in this odd little corridor — the Rossmore Corridor — between Hollywood and Hancock Park. It's a four-block stretch of old buildings that have hung on, beautifully preserved, from another era, circa 1930.

As a neighborhood, it was probably a baby conceived by developers in the Jazz Age but was born right after the crash, so it was stunted and never grew, died out after four blocks.

And now, decades and decades later, it's an island of elegance amid the blight. It's like the whole corridor could be one big version of the movie *The Shining:* all the buildings filled with beautifully dressed people from the past drinking highballs for eternity.

Yet just one block to the north of this elegant, ghostly stretch is your standard Los Angeles bleakness: six-lane thoroughfares of strip malls, gas stations, and fast-food restaurants. Nothing over two stories, just flat urban sprawl without character or beauty.

And that's where I was coming from, the north, down Vine Street, but as I crossed Santa Monica Boulevard, the Rossmore Corridor announced its spectral self in the distance, and the first tall old building I could see in the misting rain was the seven-story art deco Ravenswood. And I knew it was the Ravenswood — a spooky name if you ask me — because it has a great big lit-up sign on its roof, done up in large Germanic-looking letters.

Then beyond the Ravenswood, I could see the glowing rooftop sign of the twelve-story El Royale, which is the tallest and fairest of all the old buildings. It's the palace of the neighborhood, and its sign is famously beautiful as well: the "El" is perched above "Royale," in an elegant font, and the whole thing is done up in green neon, like the color of new money, a meretricious beacon that can be seen at a distance from all directions.

Then I crossed Melrose and was in the shrouded corridor itself. Here the road narrows and twists and changes its name, Vine becomes Rossmore, and suddenly after the flats of lower Hollywood, you're in the shadows of these beautiful tall old buildings, which form a canopy, an enclosed feeling, and it's like a movie set of a lost city.

That night, it was especially beautiful in the rain, this little preserve from another time, and halfway through the four-block corridor, I drove past the El Royale. It was on the left, on the other side of the road, and through elegant glass doors, I glimpsed its wooden golden-hued lobby, where a doorman was surely keeping guard, and I kept going. I hoped Sebastian was home, up there in his penthouse.

Then the corridor came to an end, like a tunnel ride in an amusement park.

It was no longer 1930 — I was back in 2023, whether I liked it or not — and at the stoplight, I made a left on Beverly, then a left on North Arden Boulevard, which runs parallel to Rossmore.

Using the green neon sign as my lodestar, I found the building that had its back to the El Royale. It was the St. Francis Catholic Church, which I took as a good omen. St. Francis is my favorite saint — his prayer, his thing for animals — and I drove down the church driveway to its parking lot in the back. At the end of the lot was a high concrete wall, about twelve feet, and on the other side of that wall was the backside of the El Royale.

There were a few cars in the church lot, and I noticed, as I parked the Mercury, that a metal door in the back of the church was ajar. A folding chair was propping the door open, and attached to the door handle was a circular metal sign with a triangle stenciled onto it, and inside the triangle were the letters *AA*.

It was almost nine p.m. and there must have been an AA meeting going on in the church, and a few souls, based on the cars in the lot, had ventured out in the rain to attend. I was tempted to go in there myself and get a free coffee, though I did feel some pull, beyond coffee, to check out the meeting. I've always been very fond of Alcoholics Anonymous, and I thought it might be nice to just sit there and listen and forget about my life for a little while. Years ago, I had gone to meetings and liked them very much, the coffee and the stories and the camaraderie, but I could never stay sober, which is, naturally, a big part of the AA program, and so I stopped going.

But then I found an analyst, Dr. Lavich — she was affiliated with a psychoanalytic institute that treated ex-cops for free — and I began seeing her four days a week, which proved, in my particular case, to be more effective than AA.

And it was real old-fashioned analysis: every day I'd lie on the couch, like one of Freud's patients, and Dr. Lavich, who was in her seventies, would sit behind me in her chair, listening wisely and patiently as I unraveled a lifetime of confusion and distorted thinking. She would interject when she thought it prudent, and often her dog, Janet, whom I had a crush on, which was not your usual transference, would be in her lap.

Well, the analysis really helped.

My drinking lessened considerably, almost to nothing; my suicidal ideation, which had plagued me for years, went silent; *and* I stopped having relationships, which was good for everyone involved. Dr. Lavich had said once, "Troubled people love in a troubled way."

I did meet George two years into my treatment, but that was a healthy relationship from the start, if worshipping him like a sun king is considered healthy, and, overall, the analysis was a great run-up to Buddhism. In analysis, you study your pain, take responsibility for your choices, stop acting out, and begin behaving like a rational adult. All of which could describe the Buddha's Four Noble Truths: acknowledge your pain, study your pain, stop making the same mistakes over and over, be a good person.

So I loved seeing Dr. Lavich, but then after four years on the couch, I began that horrid stretch of killing men in self-defense, in the line of my work, which culminated in fleeing to Mexico and getting the new face. But even then I couldn't escape it: I killed Diablo.

None of this, of course, was Dr. Lavich's fault or Freud's fault. I was a deeply confused person in a violent profession, and after I settled down in Dos Ballenas, I ended my analysis over email. Quite frankly, I had killed too many people to be on the couch anymore, though I didn't tell Dr. Lavich that. I simply thanked her for everything and said I had moved to Mexico. She wrote a short but sane reply — analysts are famously quite direct — and she let me know that the porch light was always on, as it were, for me to continue my treatment, should I return to LA.

And now that I was back, I did wish I could go see her and lie on the couch. But in analysis you're supposed to not censor yourself at all, otherwise it doesn't work, and I just couldn't tell Dr. Lavich what I had been up to: she might try to have me arrested. Or committed.

So there was no calling her for help, and I didn't go into the AA meeting to share my troubles. I was alone, had no one to turn to, and what I needed to do was focus and find Sebastian, and along the back wall of the church parking lot there was a large metal dumpster, which I thought I could use to my advantage.

I got out of the car with my new umbrella — it was still coming down hard — and as I approached the dumpster, which was as tall as me, I saw that leaning against it was a thickish mat, the kind that children might nap on or use for tumbling. There was a rip in it, and it had probably come from the day care at the church. I thought of lifting the dumpster lid and throwing the mat inside, things would look neater that way, but I had my own business to attend to, and I tossed my umbrella on top of the dumpster, then climbed up after it.

Standing on the dumpster, I could easily reach the top of the wall and pull myself up, but the wall, at the top, was embedded with shards of glass, in lieu of razor wire. I would get sliced to pieces, which was a problem, but then I realized I had an obvious solution. The gods had provided me with exactly what I needed — maybe because I was in a church parking lot — and I got that thick mat and draped it over the edge of the wall, over the jagged pieces of glass.

Mat in place, I glanced back at the church: no one was coming out of the AA meeting; no one had seen me. The rain was really coming down, but I closed my umbrella — it was the compact kind — and shoved it into the back of my pants.

Then I grabbed hold of the mat, which was slippery and wet, but I managed to pull myself up, and using the mat like a pommel horse, I got one leg on each side of the wall.

I was now looking at the shadowy back lot of the El Royale, which was not a parking lot, but used solely for large deliveries and for garbage trucks. There were about twenty yards of pavement between where I sat on the wall and the back of the building, enough for a truck to turn around in, and on the right side of the lot was a driveway that I knew would lead to Rossmore and a security gate.

Directly across from me was the El Royale's loading dock for moving old tenants out and new tenants in, and next to the dock was a short set of metal stairs that led to a metal back door. There was one spotlight above the loading dock, providing some meager illumination in the rain, and I saw three cameras total: two by the loading dock and one by the door. But the cameras probably didn't reach the top of the wall, where I was perched twenty yards away. At least I hoped not.

The drop to the ground was twelve feet, but directly beneath me, about six feet below, was a row of large metal dumpsters, like the one in the church lot. And I was glad to be above the dumpsters, it was better than dropping onto hard, wet pavement, slipping and breaking an ankle, but the dumpster I was above had been left open, its lid thrown back against the wall.

Inside the dumpster, there was a mass of black garbage bags and white garbage bags — the container looked to be about half full — but the light was poor, no moonlight or starlight. I just hoped there wasn't anything sharp or too disgusting in there, but I didn't have a choice. I couldn't slide the mat along the wall and get to one of the dumpsters whose lid was closed.

Still, I didn't like the idea of jumping into a pile of garbage in the rain, seemed like a bad idea, and I thought of retreating. But then how would I get into the El Royale? I could never get past the doorman, not in a building like that, and since I had come this far, I figured, *Oh, what the hell. Can't be that bad. I'll hit the garbage bags and pop right out.*

So I pushed myself off the mat, hoping for the best, and I landed in a nightmarish bog of garbage and water, and I sank all the way to my waist, half my body, and I tried to grab the lip of the dumpster, but I couldn't get purchase: my feet had perforated the garbage bags I had landed on and it was like I was standing on something alive and roiling. And the dumpster, from all the rain, had at least three feet of water in it, which I hadn't perceived from above, and there was a lot of movement in the water around my hips.

I thought there were fish in the dumpster, carp or something, which didn't make sense, but then I realized that swimming all around me in the wet darkness, as my eyes adjusted, were at least thirty or forty rats! I had landed in a drowning rat colony!

And some were trying to climb up me now to get to safety, to dry land, and I began to knock them off, utterly terrified and screaming like a banshee, and then one of them bit my hand, but that was a good thing. It was like a cattle prod, and I don't know how I did it, but I somehow launched myself out of that ratty bog, and with the panicked strength of Hercules, grabbed the edge of the dumpster and vaulted to safety.

I landed on the pavement, awkwardly, nearly twisting an ankle after all, and then I brushed at myself, like a crazy man, like Bogart in that movie where he gets covered with leeches, but no rats had made it out of the dumpster with me.

Then I had a moment of insanity, thinking there was one in my pants after all!

I shook my leg wildly and nearly took off my pants, but that was just madness that passed. I realized there was no rat, and when I started to calm down a little, I looked at my hand. It was bleeding but not terribly. The rat bite was just four little puncture wounds along the edge of the hand beneath the pinky. The pain had been more psychological than physical, and growing saner by the second, I looked about me: luckily, no one had witnessed this spectacle of a man falling into a rat-infested dumpster, and the rain had probably covered my screams. It was really pouring.

I removed my umbrella, which had made the journey and miraculously not fallen out, and I opened it, shielding myself from the downpour, not that it made much difference. I was already soaked, especially my pants and shoes. Worried, I checked my jacket pockets, but I still had my wallet and phones and all my implements, most importantly the .38.

Then I looked up: the El Royale was towering over me, twelve stories of sporadically lit windows, and at the top were the penthouses, and above that was the glowing neon-green sign.

With the umbrella shielding my face from the cameras, I crossed the twenty yards of pavement, went up the metal stairs to the back door, and put on a pair of the thin white latex gloves. In case I had to go to plan B with Sebastian — murder, not confession — it was better not to leave behind any fingerprints, and I took out my lockpick. It was a fancy building, but the lock wasn't that good, and I went through it. Then I was in a wide, roughish-looking corridor, with scuffed walls and metal doors leading to generators and furnaces and the like, and at the end of the hallway was the large service elevator.

I didn't see any cameras, but I kept my umbrella open just in case, and I walked quickly to the lift. There was a stairwell near the elevator, behind a fire door, and I thought for a moment of climbing twelve flights to Sebastian in my sopping-wet pants and shoes, but I figured there was a greater chance of running into someone on the stairs than in the elevator. It was nine o'clock at night; most of the building staff would be off duty.

I pushed the button, and the elevator was already at this level, which was the basement. Keeping the umbrella as my shield against any cameras that might be inside, I entered the wide lift, big enough for a piano, and pushed PH. Not wanting to peek out from beneath the umbrella, I couldn't be certain if there was a camera or not. It was an old building and an old lift: the service elevator might not have been hooked up to surveillance.

Nevertheless, it was a nerve-wracking two-minute ride, but no one else called for the elevator and no security stopped its progress. I made it, unimpeded, to the penthouse floor.

I stepped out of the lift, and the service elevator was housed in a separate hallway, behind a fire door, which I went through. I had my umbrella, my cloaking device, in place, and I was now in a grand beautiful hallway of dark red carpet and oak paneling. I walked past Penthouses C and D, with ornate wooden doors, and in the middle of the passageway, as I squished along, was the main elevator, whose doors were brushed gold with flowers etched onto their surface.

Then, at the end of the corridor, across from each other, were two more impressive wooden doors. One marked A and one marked B. My umbrella still very much in place, I went to B, which was on the left, and put my ear against it. I could hear music playing inside.

Sebastian was home.

With my left hand still holding the umbrella, keeping my face from being recorded by any prying cameras in the hallway, I got out my lockpick with my right hand. Underneath the quasi-translucent skin of the white latex glove, I saw that blood from the rat bite was pooling, but it didn't look too bad, and I got the lock to tumble.

Then I put the pick away, took out the .38, and went in to say hello.

12.

I OPENED AND CLOSED the door without much noise, and I was in an elegant stucco passageway with an arched ceiling. There was an old wooden door to a closet and next to that was a gold umbrella stand with two wet umbrellas in it. One of the wet umbrellas was white and feminine, and the other, your standard black umbrella, was long and pointy. Sebastian may have had company.

I closed my stubby, cheap umbrella and quietly placed it in the bucket. Seemed like the polite thing to do.

At the end of the passageway, which was covered in a Turkish rug, there was a mirror and a piece of antique furniture with a glass bowl for dropping off keys or mail. And as I cat-footed along the rug, I saw myself in the mirror and it wasn't a pretty picture: a soaking-wet madman in a black watch cap, with a gun in his white-latex hand.

Not seen in the mirror was the smell of hard-boiled eggs coming from my wet pants, courtesy of the dumpster juices I had bathed in, but it wasn't overwhelming.

The music got louder as I progressed down the hallway, and I recognized it as a song from *Buena Vista Social Club,* an album I loved, which I hadn't heard in years, and it bothered me that Sebastian would be playing it. Then the hallway turned to the right, like an elbow, and opened up to a large, dimly lit living room, which had a vaulted stucco ceiling. It also had dark-wood floors and plenty of rugs, and sitting on a leather couch, in the middle of the room, was a beautiful woman, a brunette, staring at her phone, which glowed like a bar of light.

She was in a slinky black dress and her very long legs were crossed, and in front of her, on a coffee table, was a full glass of red wine. The lighting was hushed, romantic, augmented by candles, and through the music, I could hear a shower going somewhere in the apartment, off to the left, and the woman, sensing something, looked up from her phone. Before she could scream, I was on her, my gloved hand over her mouth.

When I thought she was calm enough, I whispered, "I'm not going to hurt you," and I removed my hand. "He's in the shower?"

She nodded, mute and frightened. She smelled good and looked very expensive.

I said, "Has he already paid you?"

She glared at me with anger, her composure returning. My comment hadn't really insulted her but brought her armored shell to the surface, which was good. Meant she wouldn't scream for help. "They always pay first," she said, hard-boiled.

I took out my wallet and peeled off ten large, a thousand bucks. I handed it to her. She hesitated but took it. "Get out of here," I said.

She stood up, and I followed her to the hallway, watched her get in a raincoat and grab the white umbrella. Then she was out the door, fast. A high-priced survivor. I didn't think she would call the cops or do anything. In her position, the best thing to do was to just disappear.

I went back to the couch and took her seat. The shower was still going.

My hand was throbbing, and I quickly googled *Are rat bites serious?*

I wanted to know if I was in danger of dropping dead imminently, and what came back was a lot of information about something called, rather explicitly, rat-bite fever, which sounded terrible, but until I presented symptoms — a rash, a high fever, my throat closing — there was nothing to be done.

So I put the phone — and thoughts of the Black Death — away and picked up the prostitute's glass of wine. Wanting to be a little medically proactive, I rolled back my glove halfway and poured some of the red wine over the wound, to clean it, and then I rolled the glove back and sipped the wine. It was delicious. Hearty. Hints of the stable. Manure. Life.

And I needed it after falling into that bog.

So it was a perfect red for a cold, rainy night, when you've been bitten by a rat, and in my right hand was the .38 and in my left was the wineglass.

Maybe from nerves, I felt a little giddy and like a big shot: wait till Sebastian, that bastard, stepped into the room and saw me sitting there, drinking his wine.

Across from me, on the other side of the coffee table, was a large leather chair, and just beyond that was a partially open door, which appeared to lead to the master bedroom. It was from there that the sounds of the shower emanated, and I pointed the gun at the door to be ready.

While I waited for him, I glanced about, taking in my surroundings, and the living room I was sitting in was elegant in a masculine way: plenty of heavy old wood and leather, with the candle-glow ambiance of an expensive steak house. Everything was as tasteful as the music and the wine: he was a killer with style, spending daddy's money.

Behind me was a dining room area and a kitchen, and out the large lead-paned windows was a southward view of Los Angeles. But the city was invisible: the impenetrable mist was green from the El Royale sign, and the streaks of rain lashing the windows, also illumined by the sign, were emerald-colored and quite beautiful.

I drank about half the glass, going too fast; then the shower stopped.

A minute later, Sebastian, half naked, a white towel wrapped around his middle, came into the room. His blonde hair was wet and his knees literally buckled at the sight of me, the shock of it, and he certainly was a handsome lad: he had his mother's coloring, his father's face, and the build of an Adonis. His finger, which I had broken, was in a metal splint, and I waved the gun at him and said, "Sit down, let's talk."

He looked at me, stunned, then he knew who I was, even without the beard. His blood sugar was acting funny — his face in the hushed lighting was pale, and I thought he might faint — and he said, his voice a little trembly, "I thought you were dead. I thought you drowned that night."

I waved the gun at the leather chair on the other side of the coffee table and said, "Sit down, Sebastian. You don't look so good."

He stared at the gun in my latex hand and the glass of wine in my other hand and sat down. Regaining his front, he said, "Where's the whore?"

"Don't be rude." I took a big gulp of wine, then put it down on the coffee table and removed my phone. Keeping the gun on him, I played with the phone and got it into record mode and put it on the table between us.

I said, "I want you to tell me about Frances and why you killed her. And I also want to hear about Half Moon Bay. And how you and your father killed that girl."

His eyes widened when I said that — I had struck on something — and I knew that the recording would never stand up in court or anything like that, but if I got it into the right hands, they could start digging and put Sebastian away. Maybe his father, too.

His face reassembled quickly from his shock. Became cold. He was a cocky bastard. "You think I'm going to talk," he sneered. "I'm not going to tell you anything. You're a little man. A nothing man."

"True enough," I said, "but I think you *will* talk," and I lifted the gun and pointed it at his head, to let him know I was serious, but then the gun felt awfully heavy, wildly heavy, and I thought, *What the hell is going on? Is it the rat bite?*

Then I couldn't hold up my arm, it fell to my side, the gun dropping from my hand, and the room was starting to distort and get dim around the edges, like a fun-house mirror, and I saw Sebastian smiling at me — beautiful white teeth, such a handsome boy — and then I tried to stand, to get away from him.

But all I did was fall off the couch, I had no control over my limbs, and as I tumbled down, I saw the three-quarters-empty wineglass on the coffee table, and it hit me: he was going to roofie the prostitute, that was his thing; it was why he took his time in the shower, so she would drink the whole glass...

Then I was on the floor, and he was standing over me in his towel, a half naked, evil god. He was smiling with ridicule. "You're a fool," he said.

I am, I thought.

I said, barely a whisper, "Why did you kill Frances?"

"Because I wanted to."

Then he put his foot on my throat, to play with me, like a child sadist with an animal.

Then the Rohypnol took me away, a sudden black curtain.

13.

I CAME TO IN a car trunk, in a moving car that was strangely silent.

But I could hear the wheels on the road, the rhythmic swish through wet streets, though if I hadn't crossed the border in somewhat similar fashion, in that coffin-like container in the U-Haul van, it might have taken me longer to understand what was happening to me and where I was.

I lifted my right hand to my face—I was still wearing the latex gloves—and in the cramped, dumpster-stinky darkness, I looked at my glowing watch: it was 10:15. I had lost an hour.

But then I had a vague memory, almost like something I had seen in a movie, of Sebastian drunk-walking me to his car in the El Royale parking lot. The Rohypnol had turned me into a puppet, a zombie, and then he had put me in the trunk, maybe in case I woke up and wasn't a zombie anymore, and for some reason, he hadn't killed me. Maybe he was taking me to his father, and Calderon Sr. would decide my fate.

And I knew this was my karma for what I had done to Poole and Venturi. For forcing them to endure that eighteen-hour ride in the trunk with Felix's corpse. It was practically biblical karma, straight out of the book of Matthew: *And with what measure ye mete, it shall be measured to you again.*

Though this wasn't quite the same "measure"—this was easier than what I had put them through—it was, nevertheless, an expression of the immutable law of karma, of cause and effect, and so I felt quite accepting of being in a car trunk. It didn't strike me as unfair at all. *In fact, it's quite fair,* I reasoned in my mind.

But that wasn't just my fledgling and confused Buddhism at play.

I was high as hell from the Rohypnol; it had turned me into a Zen prisoner, and I passed back out.

* * *

I came to again, a little while later, as Sebastian was dragging me along pavement, through an opening in a wire fence. It was raining hard, with plenty of wind, and he was walking backwards, his hands under my armpits.

And as we came through the fence, he turned us a little to his right — he wasn't aware yet that I was conscious — and I saw, about fifty yards away, the Fletcher Drive Bridge, which spans the Los Angeles River in a wasteland part of the city called Frogtown.

Oh, there's the bridge, I thought, like I was in a waking dream, and it was lit up with streetlamps, glowing in the rain, and I realized we were on the bicycle path below the bridge, but twenty feet above the river. And Sebastian was dragging me to the edge of the path, to the concrete embankment, which slopes down to the water at a forty-five-degree angle.

I twisted in his arms — he knew I was awake now — and I had never seen the river so high and moving so fast, and directly in front of us, in the riverbed, half submerged, was a small copse of trees. Nature has been slowly overtaking the paving of the river sixty years ago — trees grow in the middle of it, a protest against humans turning a mighty river into a fifty-mile drainage pipe — and the noise of the rushing water that night was overwhelming, like rapids, and I understood, as I came to more and more, what Sebastian was trying to do: he was going to roll me down the sloping embankment and into the frenzied current.

I shook free then, no longer druggily compliant, and his face was above me in the downpour, ugly with rage, and he kicked me in the ribs with all he had.

"I was hoping you'd wake up," he said, "so you'd know what was happening."

I tried crawling away and got a few feet, but then he grabbed my left arm.

"Stop fighting," he said, and he started dragging me by my arm back to the edge of the embankment, and I dug my free hand into my pocket.

The paring knife was still there — Sebastian wasn't a pro; he hadn't checked my pockets for weapons — and just as he got me to the edge, I jabbed that knife deep into his thigh with all the strength of three years of ocean swimming behind it, and he screamed, a horrible shriek, like an animal, and he let go of me and tottered backwards in pain. He was trying to remove the knife from his leg, and then he disappeared. It didn't seem real, like he had been snatched, and on my belly, I peered over the concrete lip and watched him tumble down the sloping embankment, screaming all the way.

Then he was in the churning black water, and in the glow from the bridge lights, I saw him get pulled under immediately. Then he popped to the surface for a moment, fighting for his life, then he went under once more, and I didn't see him again.

Two days later, when the water level came down, his body, looking like a scarecrow, was found downstream in the branches of a barren tree.

14.

FOR ABOUT TEN MINUTES, I lay there in the cold, wind-whipped rain. Half unable to move, half in shock that I had killed again. Then, eventually, I had enough strength to stand. The roofie, which probably had been dosed for a 120-pound female, was slowly wearing off, and I went through the wire fence.

Sebastian's car, a Tesla, which accounted for its silence, was just a few feet away and still had its lights on. It was parked at the end of a dead-end street of small warehouses, and there were no streetlamps and no sign of human life. Just slanting rain. Frogtown was desolate at night. It had once been a swamp, still felt like a swamp, and it had received its colorful name when the river gave birth, ninety years ago, to a plague-like emergence of toads.

I got in the Tesla and on the front passenger seat were Venturi's gun and my phone. Sebastian must have been planning to throw them in the water after he had taken care of me.

I was still wearing the latex gloves, and since I was in his car, I kept them on, not wanting to leave behind any fingerprints. I didn't have my full IQ yet, which is no world-beater anyway, but my brains were slowly coming back, and I checked my pockets: nothing was missing. My wallet. My baton. Poole's phone. And at 10:32, Kunian had texted Poole a simple message: I'm going to kill you and that cop.

He still thought I was Shelton, still thought Poole was alive, and I looked at my watch. It was almost eleven. The night was still young. I could still make it to Riverside. I just needed some coffee.

In the meantime, I took out the two joints I had rolled back at the motel when I was getting ready for the night. They were pretty wet, but I got one lit: I wanted help figuring out my next move.

On Fletcher, a few blocks away, there was a music club called Zebulon. Or at least there was before COVID. I had been there once to hear a band. Frogtown, like a lot of city wastelands, has its hot spots, usually for music. So I thought I could go there, have a drink, and get an Uber back to my car. I didn't want an Uber to come to this dead-end street and connect me with the Tesla.

Then I had a feeling that the car, which was silent, was on. I had never been in a Tesla before — the ceiling was interesting, like the glass of an indoor pool at a cheap hotel — and I put my foot down on the pedal and the instrument panel responded accordingly. The car was in park but definitely on. I looked at the center console: Sebastian's phone was plugged into the dash, and I wondered if the phone was acting like a key to the car. That as long as the phone was in the car, I could drive it.

I picked up the phone and it was open, maybe because it was connected to the Tesla. I went into Settings and removed the need for a passcode. Then I went into Contacts and found "Dad." Which seemed an odd choice of word for a sociopath to use about his father, but I don't know how these things work. Maybe Sebastian had some normal feelings mixed in there.

The good news was, I now had access to Vincente Calderon. His private number. And a plan was starting to form in my mind. I turned the car around, made a right on a street called Ripple, which was lined with squat warehouses, and went up to Fletcher Drive.

At Fletcher, I made a left, skipped Zebulon, and drove another half mile, passing underneath the 5 freeway, and went to the Astro diner, which is open twenty-four hours.

I really needed coffee.

15.

THE OLDER GREEK MAN at the front gave me the hairy eyeball — I was soaking wet — but I ignored him and went to a booth without asking to be seated. The restaurant was empty, just one man at the wood-colored Formica counter, eating scrambled eggs and looking at his phone. But that was the only modern touch to the place: the Astro is as old-school as they come, been around since 1960 and looks it.

The long counter has swively chairs covered in orange imitation leather and there are a bunch of booths, also covered in fake leather. The windows, which are old tinted plastic and resemble the roof of a Tesla, look out onto Silver Lake Boulevard and Fletcher, and the place comes with a menu that's as thick as a phone book, but there isn't much that's safe to eat.

The waitress, an old Mexican woman, arrived and sniffed the air. I still had some dumpster perfume on me, but most of it had been washed off when I lay on the ground in the rain. She said, "What happened to you? Did you fall into the river?" She didn't offer me the thick menu she held.

"Just about," I said. "But my money is dry." I took out my wallet and the money wasn't that dry. But I didn't want her and the maître d', who was watching us, to think I was a homeless wet bum, looking to get warm, which I sort of was. I took out a damp twenty to show her I was for real and said, "I don't need a menu. I'll have a coffee and a bowl of chicken noodle."

She looked at me with pity and went off to the kitchen.

I went to the bathroom and washed my rat bite with soap.

I had taken off the latex gloves in the parking lot and my hand was swollen along the edge, but I could still use a gun. I went back to the booth.

First coffee and soup, and then I would start putting my plan into action.

* * *

After my little meal, which included four cups of black coffee, I stood under the overhang of the Astro's front door and texted Calderon Sr. on Sebastian's phone: Dad, call me. It's an emergency. The rain was much calmer now, just a light drizzle, and after two minutes the Sinaloa lawyer called his dead son. I answered, said, "Hi, Dad."

After a beat, he said, wary, "Who is this?"

"We met earlier today. You didn't like me. Your wife was drunk."

He was silent. Then, with fear in his voice: "How do you have my son's phone?"

"That's a good question. Here's another question: You want to see Sebastian alive again?"

He was silent, then said, cold, "Do you know who I am?"

"I have an idea. Which is why I know you can do what I'm going to ask of you. For a quarter million, you get pretty boy back in one piece, and that'll also buy my silence on the girl down in Mexico and the one you had killed up in Half Moon Bay."

He didn't say anything, but I had baited the hook pretty good.

Then I told him where to go and what time I expected him.

16.

I took an Uber, using Poole's phone, back over to the St. Francis church. I didn't think the Tesla was safe to drive: I figured that kind of car could be tracked, especially if it was on. Which was why I also turned off Sebastian's phone. His father might be able to track that as well. But if it was off, I was probably all right. For a little while, anyway. And I wasn't ready yet to destroy the phone. I still needed it.

Back in the Mercury, I left the church parking lot a little after midnight, stopped at a 76 gas station on Santa Monica Boulevard, and got a large coffee to add to the four coffees I'd had at the Astro: I was working hard to counteract the tranquilizer I had been slipped.

Then I was back in the car and driving to Riverside.

I was on caffeine, weed, and the trippy remnants of the Rohypnol, and I drove in a hyperfocused, monofixated way, without any music, and turned into the driveway of the garden store, next to the strip club, at 1:45.

I parked in the back by the concrete wall, which was the border between the two properties, and the ladder that had been leaning against the store was gone. I got out of the car, frantic to find it — it was essential to my half-cocked plan — and luckily it was lying alongside some wooden packing crates. I leaned it back against the building, and there was still just a light drizzle, which seemed like nothing after thirty-six hours of mostly hard rain.

I got back into the car, put Sebastian's phone on, and called his father. He answered by saying, "I want to speak to my son."

"You will. When I have the money. You gonna be on time?"

"…Yes." It sounded like he was in a car, en route. This was good.

"If you're late," I said, "I kill him. I like money but I like being alive more."

I hung up the phone and turned it off. Then I took out Poole's phone. Called Kunian. He answered: "Where the fuck are you?"

"On my way to see you."

He was silent. Then: "Who is this?"

"You know who. Poole's dead."

"You! You fucking bastard!! I'm gonna kill you. Gut you like a fucking fish! You hear me, you motherfucker?"

I let him vent. Then I said, "I have a crazy proposition for you. I want to buy my freedom."

"What the fuck are you talking about?"

"I scored big. Ripped off a Sinaloa mule. I'll give you a quarter million cash. That should settle things between us, and you take the bounty off my head."

"What the fuck are you talking about?"

"I'm talking about buying my freedom. Meet me in your parking lot, behind the club, at three. This is no joke."

"Are you crazy?"

"I'm sick of looking over my shoulder. A quarter million. I'm gonna be there at three. You can have your boys with you. I'm going to come in alone. But I'll have a bunch of hitters from the LAPD who'll be on the street. I don't come back out, they come in."

He knew I was full of shit, but I could hear in his silence that he was curious what this play would actually be. Then he said, "You're crazy."

"Just be in the parking lot at three. You'll get the money. You can wait in your car. But I think the rain won't be so bad."

Then I hung up and turned the phone off.

It was a crazy plan, but I thought no matter what, something bad would happen, which in this case would be good. Both men would know it was a screwed-up trap of some kind, but they'd have to see it through, especially Calderon.

He had probably sent men to the El Royale and maybe they had tracked the Tesla to the Astro. But it didn't matter. They weren't going to find Sebastian, so Calderon would have to believe that I had his son. Plus, I had told him things I shouldn't know, about Baja and Half Moon Bay, which were more fires for him to put out, besides saving his son, and so I had forced his hand. I'd left him no choice but to come, and I was counting on his bringing a small army.

As for Kunian, he might not stick his neck out and be in the parking lot, but if things went the way I hoped, it would be fine if he stayed hidden in the club. Calderon was going to tear the place apart looking for Sebastian, looking for me, and I didn't think Kunian would come out of there alive.

That was the idea, anyway, and I had about an hour to kill. I had wanted to give Calderon enough time to get things together, or more accurately the illusion of getting things together, and I tilted back the seat. I lit up my last joint and closed my eyes.

But it wasn't good to relax. I dropped some kind of internal guard in my mind, and I flashed to Sebastian tumbling down the embankment to his death, and an icy feeling came over me. *I had killed again.* It really hit me, and I started shaking bad. I put the car back on and ran the heater, but the shaking wouldn't stop. It was a delayed stress reaction, and I felt like I was on the verge of a seizure, my limbs going all nuts.

Then I split.

I was in the passenger seat looking at the guy in the driver's seat.

I didn't know who he was, but I didn't like him. Didn't like his face.

Then my two bodies became one body again, and I started rocking, while smoking, to soothe myself. The rocking put me back in control, and I did the math in my head. Diablo had been number eight. Then if you counted Poole and Venturi, whom I passively killed by leaving to die in a car trunk, that was nine and ten, and now Sebastian was eleven. Eleven human beings! The worst sin you could commit, and I had done it eleven times now!

Which was maybe why I had concocted this trap. Let other people get their hands bloodied. I couldn't take it anymore. But killing still needed to be done, because I was in an upside-down world, where the worst solution was the only solution. Or so it seemed. I just hoped this would bring things to an end, like a cleansing fire, like a forest fire.

Then I realized where the idea for this scheme had originated. I had unconsciously stolen the premise of Justin Kearse's film *The Woods:* I was getting other people to do my killing, like the serial killer in his movie, and I laughed strangely, some kind of weird vocalization. Then I picked up the pace of my rocking, which I had done as a boy in my room.

All my life I have felt like I've done something wrong — something I can't quite remember — and that a terrible punishment is imminent. From earliest childhood, I have lived with this sensation, this paranoia, and I tried to put a dent in it with my analysis, but in the end, like a capitulation, I had created a life to match a phantom feeling. Eleven times I did *do* something terribly wrong.

And punishment *was* imminent.

I finished the joint and passed the time just rocking. It was a great skill from childhood. I could disappear for hours doing it. It made life bearable. Then as now.

At 2:45, I got out of the car and climbed the ladder up to the roof of the gardening store.

The rain had finally stopped, just like the DJ on 88.5 had said it would.

There was a three-foot-high lip around the roof that I could squat behind, unseen, and from there I had a perfect view of the Diamond Dancers parking lot. The place had closed at two and there were only three cars at the very back of the lot, facing out: two black Chevy Suburbans and a silver Mercedes. There was also a dumpster, not as big as the one I had fallen into, and I wondered if there were rats drowning inside.

I turned on Poole's phone and called Kunian. He answered: "You coming?"

"See you in fifteen minutes in the parking lot and you'll get your money. Quarter mil. Forget the blood feud, this is business."

Then I hung up and turned the phone off.

At 2:50, a man who looked like the bouncer came out of a hatch on the roof of the strip club and lay down by the edge, pointing an AK-47 at the lot. He didn't see me across the way on the opposite roof, which was half a story higher: he was looking down, not up. I kept my head low anyway.

Then Kunian and Stevie, who had a bandage on his nose, came out of a back entrance of the club and went into one of the Suburbans, and they were followed by Stevie's older brother, who had a shotgun. The brother hid himself behind the dumpster.

Kunian, like a real sucker, had fallen completely for my ruse. His curiosity had been too great. It was like being told not to look at the sun and so you look at the sun.

Then I activated Sebastian's phone, called his father.

He answered: "Let me speak to Sebastian."

"Soon enough. I'm in a Suburban in the back of the lot. Pull up, don't come closer than ten feet. Then come out with the money, drop it in front of my car, walk back to your car, and I'll send your kid out."

Before he could say anything, I hung up.

He showed up a minute later, eight minutes early.

He was in the black Lincoln Navigator I'd seen at his house, and it came flying into the lot with the DEA Impala right behind it. Then the Impala pulled even with the Navigator, and they were facing the Suburban, about fifteen feet away. Nobody moving. I got the .38 out of my pocket and called Calderon Sr. He answered, like a broken record: "I want to speak with my son. I don't see him in the car. There's an old man and somebody else."

"He's in the back with me. Step out of the Lincoln with the money or I'm going to blow his head off right now. Tell the DEA pricks not to do anything."

I hung up and the DEA agent, Xavier, stepped out of the Lincoln with a small carry-on suitcase. His partner must have been driving the Impala, and he had been riding with Calderon, playing the lackey, and I let him take two steps, and then I fired twice at Kunian's Suburban, hitting the hood of the car. This set things off good, and Stevie's brother stepped out from behind the dumpster, shot Xavier with the shotgun, and he flopped to the ground, dead, and the man on the roof, the bouncer, lit into the Lincoln with the automatic rifle.

Then Xavier's partner was out of the Impala, shielding himself behind his door, and he started firing at Stevie's brother by the dumpster and the brother went down.

This got Stevie out of the Suburban, and he was firing from behind his door at the agent, and it was a gunfight all right, and then three more Lincolns came flying into the lot, Calderon's backup, but I saw Calderon, bloodied from the AK-47 strafing his car, get out and make a run for it, panicking, but the bouncer on the roof saw him and shot him in the head.

Then somebody from the backup crew lit up the bouncer and he dropped, and only Stevie was left. Now all the firepower coming from Calderon's men was directed at Kunian's Suburban, and Stevie went down, and Kunian tried to get away, made it two feet from the car. But then he was shot multiple times, fell face-first to the ground, DOA, and that was my cue: I scurried down the ladder, got to the Mercury, and floored it out of there.

Five minutes later, not followed by anyone, I pulled onto a residential side street and tossed Sebastian's phone, Poole's phone, and the gun into a sewer.

Then I put the Hollywood Downtowner Motel into the GPS.

George and Walter were waiting for me back in the room.

17.

WHEN I GOT TO Hollywood around 4:30, what I really wanted was
another bath, while smoking a joint, and because I'm a terrible pothead
and had caused a lot of death that night, I went to the house to get some
more weed, my medicine, before going back to the motel.

I parked on the street instead of in my garage, figuring I'd be in and out,
and I climbed the stairs, having to brush away the tree branches, still heavy
with water.

I went in the front door, flicked on the lights, and Poole and Venturi
were standing there, waiting for me, guns out.

Déjà vu from Mexico.

They looked like shit but were alive.

On the table where I eat my meals, I saw an iPad. Venturi's iPad, which
had been in his bag. I knew in that instant that he had used it to track his
cell phone, which I had left on, in my house, leading them right to me.
Before I could reach for my baton, Poole shot me in the leg: his gun, a .22,
had a silencer.

It didn't put a huge hole in my thigh, it was only a .22, but it still hurt
like hell, and I went down to my knees. Venturi then kicked me in the
head, and I collapsed onto my stomach. Poole put his foot on my
neck — twice in one night this had happened, weird how things go that
way sometimes, like a run in cards — and Venturi grabbed my wrists and

cuffed my hands behind me, pulling the zip real tight. He said, "Not going to make that mistake this time, you fucker. Three days in a fucking Mex hospital because of you, you bitch."

I was in a lot of pain but managed to say, "Welcome to my home, fellas."

Venturi then yanked me to my feet, and I was able to stand. The wound in my leg wasn't that bad. Poole, his scar livid on his cheek, spit in my face, then said, spitting some more, "We're going to throw you in the trunk, give you a taste of what you put us through."

So I was right: my time in Sebastian's trunk hadn't been equal measure, not bad enough karma, but now I wondered about *their* karma. I had told them if they escaped from the trunk that they weren't to do this, that their karma would be twice as bad, but I figured I must have been wrong. I said, "How did you get out?"

Poole's answer was to hit me across the face with the .22, but Venturi said, "A friend of the doctor's showed up the next morning. You left the keys, you idiot."

I hadn't thought to take them, it was true, and they marched me out of the house, not wasting any time and not knowing that their money was two feet away in the kitchen wall, money intended for Felix's widow. They clearly hadn't gone home yet. They had come straight from the border.

We started down the steps — I was in front of them, limping from the bullet in my leg — and I said, "Where you taking me?"

"Kunian," said Poole. "He's gonna pay nicely for you, you sick fuck."

"He doesn't know we're coming?"

"Not yet. We wanted to make sure we had you."

"Makes sense," I said, and I thought of how I had watched Kunian die ninety minutes ago, and as for me, this was it. No illusion of reprieve. I was out of Houdini moves. I just hoped George and Walter would be all right, that the manager at the motel would read my note. But I knew I was getting what I deserved: the terrible punishment I had been waiting for all my life.

Then, halfway down the steps, there was the most incredible noise, a great explosion of some kind. I had never heard anything so loud, and I was suddenly flying through the air, in tremendous pain, and I thought, *Poole shot me in the back of the head, that's what's happened. I'm dead.*

A few hours later, I came to, and it was no longer night. There was sunlight, though it wasn't quite reaching me. I was flat on my face at the bottom of my stairs, covered in tree.

The mighty hundred-foot eucalyptus, after thirty-six hours of rain, had had enough. It had become too waterlogged, snapped at its base, and toppled. The tree had missed my house but had slashed across my yard and went down my staircase, and as it died, it had screamed, a scream that had been building for a hundred years.

At the end of its fall, it had knocked out my wooden fence, sent it into the street, and so I slithered on my belly out from under the enormous eucalyptus until I hit the ground ivy and weeds that are at the front of my property. From there, because the fence was gone, I was able to roll down to the road.

It must have been around 6:30 in the morning, and the sun was magnificent.

Los Angeles is at its most beautiful after a rain.

I managed to get to my feet. Somehow, I was still alive. But that was me in a nutshell. Like when I was in the ring in the Navy: *easy to hit, hard to put down.* That should be on my gravestone. If I ever have one.

I went to my closest neighbor, on the left, and kicked at their door, since my hands were bound behind me. I woke them up and they saw me through the peephole and wouldn't come out. Later, at the hospital, I would see my face and understand why. But they at least called the police. And all the services arrived.

The firefighters found Venturi and Poole beneath the tree. Venturi had died during the night, but Poole, both his legs broken, was still alive, barely, and was put next to me in the back of the EMT van. We were both on stretchers and our eyes met and a pink blood bubble rose from his lips, like a kid with chewing gum. I think he was trying to tell me something. Probably not anything nice.

A few minutes later he died. Karma. I had tried to warn him.

All told, it was estimated that the storm had taken eighteen lives, and I was never sure if Sebastian Calderon, Lucas Poole, and Marco Venturi were part of that tabulation.

But I knew that the storm had killed them. *With my help.*

I was out of Hollywood Presbyterian by noon — I left against medical advice — and I rushed to the motel. But George, being the hero that he is, hadn't done anything in the room! I quickly leashed him and took him for a walk, and he relieved himself copiously, without a single complaint.

I was limping from my gunshot wound as we walked, but I wasn't in pain. They had given me a shot of morphine at the hospital, which was better than any joint I could have ever rolled.

When we got back to the room, I looked at myself in the mirror.

It truly was a miracle that I wasn't killed — maybe the eucalyptus tree, as the guardian of the slope, had come to my aid — but, nevertheless, I had landed on my face quite forcefully, and all the doctor's work back in Mexico had been undone.

I had broken my nose, both eye sockets, and my left cheekbone. My puffed eyes were weird, bloody slits, and my very swollen face was many colors — green, yellow, red, black — but I could see beneath the massive swelling and strange coloration that when I healed this would be an entirely new face. Maybe closer to the original. Which made sense. Things always come full circle in life. You end up where you began. Maybe you never leave.

I put out the DO NOT DISTURB sign, stripped off my clothes, and got between the crisp motel sheets. I was desperate to sleep, but it was the middle of the day and even with the curtains, it was still very light in the room.

So I wrapped a towel around my eyes, like Oedipus, to help block out the light, and thinking about Oedipus brought Dr. Lavich to mind, and I thought maybe I would give her a call after all. Maybe I wasn't beyond repair and could resume my treatment.

But I quickly dismissed that notion. She would still have me arrested. Analysts have firm boundaries. Then I thought of Monica. After my face healed, I'd go to the Dresden for that drink. I could be her barfly again and maybe... *maybe*...

But I knew that was the morphine talking, and so I got all snuggled in the cool bed, my eyes bandaged from the world. It was time to rest, and George was by my heart, and Walter was above my head, like a crown.

And I felt happy to be alive.

Then that feeling passed, but it was nice while it lasted.

ACKNOWLEDGMENTS

I would like to thank and acknowledge Stephanie Davis, Eric Simonoff, and Anne Thornton for their unflagging and kind support during the writing of the Doll series (with more Doll books to come, I hope). I would also like to express my gratitude and thanks to Josh Kendall and Liv Ryan and everyone at Mulholland Books and Little, Brown and Company for their excellent and hard work on the three Doll novels.

ABOUT THE AUTHOR

Jonathan Ames is the author of several books, including *Wake Up, Sir!* and, most recently, *The Wheel of Doll* and *A Man Named Doll*. His novels *The Extra Man* and *You Were Never Really Here* have been adapted into films, and he's the creator of two television series, *Blunt Talk* and *Bored to Death*.